CHAPTER ONE

"I HOPE NO ONE MINDS us parking here."

Dorothy Murdock glanced at Jasmine Storm, her less than enthusiastic passenger, before pulling her car behind a wooden garage in a dark alley half a block from the public library. A door slammed on the opposite side of the alley just after she turned off the ignition. Footsteps sounded on wooden steps, and then a few seconds later it was quiet.

"I'm sure someone will investigate if they have a problem," Jasmine said. Then maybe Dorothy would give up her quest and go home. "You know it's very possible that nothing will happen tonight."

"I have nothing better to do."

Jasmine sent her boss a disbelieving look. "You have about five hundred projects going."

"I want to find out how the library is getting unlocked, who is doing it and why."

"I still think the chances of the person who's responsible coming by tonight are slim." Jasmine frowned over at Dorothy. "You don't plan on doing this every night, do you?"

"Of course not."

Jasmine wasn't certain she believed her. Dorothy

might be a librarian by trade and have put more than thirty years into the profession, but she was an adventurer at heart. Jasmine was not. She was careful. She saved her money, invested in retirement, looked both ways before she crossed the street. She was neither a mystery solver nor a risk taker.

But she was tonight. She couldn't let a sixty-year-old woman do surveillance by herself in a dark alley—not that anything was going to happen.

Dorothy pulled a package of chocolate-chip cookies from her tote bag and offered a cookie to Jasmine, who shook her head. The car was getting stuffy, and after a brief discussion they decided to crack open the windows and avoid conversation.

For the next hour Dorothy sipped bottled water and Jasmine stared out the window at the dark library, trying to remember the last time she'd been so bored, and occasionally reminding herself that it was no one's fault but her own that she was there watching Dorothy's back. Dorothy would have happily conducted her stakeout alone.

At eleven-thirty, Jasmine started to nod off in spite of her efforts to the contrary, when Dorothy gasped. Jasmine sat upright and squinted into the darkness, her heart beating faster.

"Over there…by the shrubbery…something moved."

"Probably a big dog," Jasmine whispered, rolling her sore shoulders. But then she saw it, too, and froze. A dark form, definitely human, slipping through the shadows toward the library. Her breath caught, not out of fear of the person, but out of fear of what Dorothy might do next. The little woman was practically quivering with anticipa-

She opened her door
to a tired-looking cop

He couldn't have gotten more than a few hours' sleep, but there he was, wearing the faded blue jeans and dark T-shirt that appeared to be his standard off-duty wardrobe.

Jasmine looked past Tony to the truck parked at the curb with a mattress and box spring in the back and a giant dog in the cab.

"*That's* your dog?"

"I told you he was big."

"That's not big. That's economy size."

He laughed, and she felt the impact of the unexpected transformation. He was surprisingly attractive when he wasn't being condescending or annoying.

"You're sure about this? Having me move in?" he asked, the laughter fading from his face.

This was probably the last time he'd give her an out.

Her last chance to bail.

Dear Reader,

Okay, I'll admit it—I love heroes with a bit of tarnish on them. Men who have not always made the best choices, and who do not always conform to societal norms, but are, in their own way, hero material. Under their rough exteriors, these are decent men who have a lot to offer—usually more than they realize.

Tony DeMonte is just such a guy—a cynical, burned-out undercover cop who lives with a dog he rescued from a drug dealer and has no idea what his next step in life will be. He's the perfect foil for librarian Jasmine Storm. A woman with a predatory, dog-hating cat, Jasmine organizes her life as a hobby. But opposites truly do attract, and when Tony and his dog move into Jasmine's basement apartment, she comes to the amazing conclusion that her annoying, irreverent and surprisingly hunky tenant may just be a keeper— and that she may not be the play-it-safe woman she always thought she was.

I hope you enjoy reading about Tony, Jasmine, Ghengis Khat and Muttzilla as much as I enjoyed writing about them. I love hearing from readers, so please drop me a line at www.jeanniewrites.com.

Happy reading,

Jeannie Watt

COP ON LOAN
Jeannie Watt

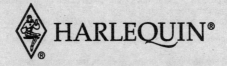

HARLEQUIN®

TORONTO • NEW YORK • LONDON
AMSTERDAM • PARIS • SYDNEY • HAMBURG
STOCKHOLM • ATHENS • TOKYO • MILAN • MADRID
PRAGUE • WARSAW • BUDAPEST • AUCKLAND

ISBN-13: 978-0-373-71520-6
ISBN-10:   0-373-71520-X

COP ON LOAN

www.eHarlequin.com

Printed in U.S.A.

ABOUT THE AUTHOR

Jeannie Watt lives with her husband in an isolated area of northern Nevada, and teaches junior-high science in a town forty miles away from her home. She lives off the grid in the heart of ranch country, and considers the battery-operated laptop to be one of the greatest inventions ever. When she is not writing, Jeannie likes to paint, sew and feed her menagerie of horses, ponies, dogs and cats. She has degrees in geology and education.

Books by Jeannie Watt

HARLEQUIN SUPERROMANCE

Don't miss any of our special offers. Write to us at the following address for information on our newest releases.

Harlequin Reader Service
U.S.: 3010 Walden Ave., P.O. Box 1325, Buffalo, NY 14269
Canadian: P.O. Box 609, Fort Erie, Ont. L2A 5X3

tion. Jasmine got ready to tackle her if she had to in order to keep her from exiting the car and defending her library.

The person moved closer to one of the library doors and Dorothy sat up straighter, craning her neck to see. The form stilled, and then it turned and darted back the way it'd come, around the corner of the building, out of sight.

Dorothy reached for the door handle.

"Don't even think about it," Jasmine ordered.

"But I recognized—" Dorothy abruptly stopped speaking and her eyes grew round as she stared over Jasmine's shoulder.

Mystified, Jasmine followed Dorothy's gaze and then her heart hit her ribs as she found herself staring down the business end of a very, *very* big gun.

"Police," the man said in a low voice. "Don't move."

TONY DEMONTE WAS TIRED and he was pissed—more for his partner than for himself. Yates had spent weeks trying to put together a bust—his first—and now some vigilante neighbor had blown it sky-high by calling to tell Dispatch that if the police didn't do something about the drug house, then he and his buddies were going to. Tonight. And they were going to start with the car parked in the alley, waiting to buy.

Tony understood people wanting to clean up their neighborhoods, but it would have been a damn sight more effective if Yates had been able to work on his own time frame. And now, since the house had been amazingly devoid of anything drug related, it appeared as though the dealer had been spooked by the car that had been sitting in the alley for so long.

Which left the question, what in the hell had these

women been doing parked behind a suspected drug dealer's house for several hours?

Yates motioned for the driver, a woman about sixty, to step to the other side of the unmarked patrol car, leaving the passenger to Tony.

"Do you have some identification?" he asked the woman.

"In my wallet."

"Go ahead and get that out."

Her hand was shaking as she removed her driver's license and then handed it out to him.

Oh, well. If you choose to hang out in alleys, you need to be prepared for the consequences.

He compared the ID with the woman standing in front of him. Straight brown hair, brown eyes. Her height and weight matched the description. She actually looked better in the photo than she did in person, but he attributed that to rampant anxiety and bad lighting in the alley.

"Is this your real name?"

"Excuse me?" The question seemed to startle her.

"Jasmine Storm. Is it your real name?"

"Of course it's my real name. Why wouldn't it be?"

"It sounds like a stripper name."

Her eyes widened and Tony sensed that he may have offended her.

"It's my *real* name."

"It's a nice one. Why are you here?"

She drew herself up. "I'm a library technician—"

"You're a *librarian?*" *Oh, man.*

"Library technician. It's different. The library is right there."

"I know where the library is."

"We were here to find out how the basement door gets unlocked."

She spoke grudgingly, as if not wanting to admit to such a ridiculous activity, and Tony started counting the painful throbs now beating in his temple.

"The door's locked when we leave at night, but in the morning it's unlocked."

There was a silence and he realized the story was over. He rubbed hand across his face. "That's maybe the stupidest thing I've heard all day."

"It's the truth," she snapped.

"Doesn't make it any less stupid."

Jasmine Storm glared at him. "Are you a real police officer?"

"No," he said blandly, "these guys let me hang out with them if I promise to buy the beer after their shift."

"I want to see a badge."

He picked up the shield attached to the chain around his neck, held it out for her to see, then dropped it again.

"I didn't get the number."

"Would it make a difference?"

"It will when I report you."

Ah, so the librarian was going to play hardball—or try to. *Good luck.*

"The name is Anthony DeMonte. There's only one of me on the force, so no one should have a problem figuring out who you're reporting." And he didn't really care if she did, because he was an official short-timer. Seven weeks.

"They're probably used to it."

He shifted gears. "Were you aware that the house you parked behind is a possible drug locale?"

"I'm aware now."

She would have to be pretty dense not to be, since the bust of a bust had occurred within seconds of Yates's identifying himself and keeping her and the older lady contained while the rest of the team swarmed the place. If the raid itself hadn't tipped her off, then Yates forgetting himself and cursing about the absence of drugs should have clinched the matter.

"How about before?"

"Why would I be… I mean, this house is only four doors down from the library. I never dreamed…"

Most people in nicer, quiet neighborhoods didn't.

"You didn't find anything, though, did you?"

That's it, honey. Touch the sore spot. He glanced over at the house. "I can't say." *Translation: Not even a pipe.*

Still, Yates was positive that Robert Davenport, the man who owned the house they had just raided, as well as several others in the neighborhood, was knee-deep in the drug trade. If that was true, then it was only a matter of time before things were in operation again. And then maybe Yates would have some vindication. Tony hoped so.

"Stay here." He walked over to Yates, who'd just given the other woman permission to inspect the library door.

"Librarians?"

Yates nodded. "Apparently, they've been having some trouble with someone breaking into the library, and decided to sit in the alley and see what happened."

"Same story I got."

"I know that one." Yates pointed at the older lady. "Her name's Dorothy Murdock. She did story hour when I was a kid."

Vigilante citizens and vigilante librarians. What next? Tony muttered an impolite word.

"Guess we can turn them loose."

"Guess so."

He walked back to where Jasmine Storm waited, and Yates headed back to Dorothy Murdock.

"Take my advice and stay out of alleys. Get a surveillance camera if you want to watch the doors," Tony said.

"We can go?"

"Yes."

She glanced past him to the back of the library, where Dorothy Murdock was now inspecting the lock with a flashlight, Yates by her side, and then focused on Tony once again.

"Your treatment of me tonight was less than professional, you know."

Tony's eyebrows went up in surprise. "You're critiquing my performance?"

"Yes, I am," she said, straightening her shoulders. "Is it standard procedure to tell people they're stupid and they have stripper names?"

"I didn't mean to offend you," he said in his cop voice. "Please accept my apologies."

She pulled open the car door without answering, so he tried one more time. "Lady, I'm tired."

"So am I, and I haven't been rude to you."

"Tell you what. I'll give you one free shot to make up for it. Go ahead. Be rude to me. You'll feel better."

Jasmine suddenly narrowed her eyes, as though she'd solved a problem that had been niggling at her. "I know you."

Tony frowned. "No, you—"

"I've seen you at the little market. More than once."

Tony studied her, shook his head. He did shop at a little market, and maybe she had seen him there…but he couldn't recall her.

As her expression changed, he realized that a smart man probably didn't admit to things like that, even silently.

"I'll say hello next time," she said with a little sneer, and then she got in the car.

He tried to think of something to say, but came up with nothing except for a brilliant, "Yeah. You do that."

AFTER DOROTHY HAD DROPPED her at her home, Jasmine shut the front door and leaned back against it, exhaling loudly. She was embarrassed and exhausted.

The things that had happened tonight never happened to people like her. She sincerely hoped they'd never happen again.

Dorothy had been apologetic on the drive home, but Jasmine suspected that her boss had found the events of the evening stimulating and perhaps even entertaining. Jasmine had not.

She'd had a gun pointed at her, been accused of attempting to buy drugs, and then insulted by an intense and decidedly unprofessional police officer—one who shopped in her little market. All in all, an extraordinary Friday night.

She needed a cup of tea.

Jasmine was halfway to the kitchen, when she heard the characteristic thud of her tabby, Ghengis Khat, landing on the outside windowsill—his cue that he wanted in. Jasmine stopped. He was already supposed to be in.

She distinctly remembered blocking his escape with one foot as she had closed the door on her way out.

Or at least, she *thought* she distinctly remembered it. Maybe the stressful evening had caused her to lose her grasp on reality. And Ghengis *was* getting slipperier in his quest to roam the neighborhood at will, terrorizing small animals. She'd have to be more careful, especially after that last incident involving Peaches, the poodle next door.

The big cat stalked into the house as soon as Jasmine opened the door, looking decidedly put out—a sure sign that she should check the answering machine.

The light wasn't blinking.

Thank goodness. Whatever her cat had been up to, it had, for once, gone unnoticed.

"DAVENPORT IS LAUGHING AT ME."

Yates was not taking his failed bust well. He'd gone to high school with Robert Davenport, a former track star who'd been kicked off the team for dealing dope his junior year. Yates had been the one who'd turned him in, and Davenport had not forgotten or forgiven.

Ten years had passed, and Davenport now owned and rented out several houses in the neighborhood of the library, while he himself lived in a ritzier area of town on the hill above the river. He drove a nice car, spent a lot of money—all supposedly obtained through the electronics business he ran out of a small storefront in the seamier part of town—but Yates was convinced that he was actually a drug-dealing middleman, who received the dope in quantity and then bagged it for resale.

Yates hadn't been able to get anything on Davenport

himself, but after talking long and hard, he'd convinced a judge that there was sufficient cause to believe that one of the man's rentals was a drug house and a warrant was in order.

Tony knew that Yates had been hoping to find both dope and some miracle piece of evidence that would link everything irrefutably to his nemesis, but he would have settled for dope.

It hadn't worked out that way—in fact the house had been eerily clean. The tenants hadn't looked all that scummy either and Tony mentioned that to Yates as they settled at a table with a pitcher of beer.

"No. They looked smart. Smart and smug," Yates said as he filled his glass, careless of how much head he put on the beer. "I thought we'd find *something* in the house. But then, they had about an hour to clear everything out while the ladies sat out back." Yates lifted the pitcher toward Tony's glass, but Tony shook his head and reached for it himself, preferring to have beer in his glass rather than foam.

"And transport it where, without someone seeing the move?" Tony asked.

Yates shook his head.

The men were quiet for a moment, each focused on his own thoughts, and then Tony shook his head. "Damn," he said. "Busting librarians. What are the odds?"

"I don't want to talk about it."

Yates called it a night after his second beer, leaving Tony to finish the pitcher alone. He didn't mind. Yates had a wife waiting at home. All Tony had was a big dog he'd inherited from a drug dealer several months ago. Being temporary, he hadn't worked to forge any bonds or make any friends in the department—in fact, his friendship with Yates had been accidental.

He had nothing in common with the eager-beaver, occasionally clumsy young cop, but after working together on a buy-bust operation Tony was directing—being a master of the art—they'd found they didn't mind each other's company. Yates wanted to know about Tony's undercover job, and Tony enjoyed talking to someone who was still passionate about policing in the way Tony had once been, before reality had sucked all the glamour out of the job.

His current position, filling in for an injured officer in Mondell, a town a couple of hundred miles from Seattle, had been a godsend after the last assignment—a grueling and near-fatal guns-for-dope undercover operation. The small-town assignment was also an opportunity for a breather and to get perspective while drawing a paycheck.

Tony was still waiting for the perspective to kick in but sensed he was getting closer. At least he'd made a career decision. He was going back to narcotics.

When he'd first arrived in Mondell, still dealing with the fallout from his last long undercover job, he'd planned to apply for the patrol job slated to open up in his Seattle department soon after this temporary assignment was done. He had ten years to go before he could retire with the required thirty years on the job, and patrol would be a quieter way to spend the remainder of his career. But after a few weeks in Mondell, he'd realized that he'd become too free-form in his methods to be comfortable in the confines of patrol.

And he wasn't so certain he was cut out for dealing

with the public, either, as his run-in with the librarian demonstrated. Mondell was a peaceful university town located on the banks of the Sitkum River, and, with the exception of a brisk drug trade, it represented a different, more laid-back world than the one Tony had become accustomed to. He felt oddly out of place there, or maybe just out of kilter dealing with the citizenry, as if he'd spent so much time on the dark side of life that he was ill-prepared to operate on the light side.

Tony swallowed his beer, then tipped his head back to lean against the wall behind him, letting his eyelids half shut as he studied the other patrons—a habit he couldn't shake. Clearly, he needed to get back to his old job, but he'd approach it differently, more sanely, take fewer chances, avoid the adrenaline rush when he could…if that was possible.

The constant stress had started to wear on him over the years, though all in all, he was doing all right. Unlike his occasional partner and former friend, Gabe, who popped in and out of rehab the way other people went to the grocery store—hovering on the brink of total self-destruction and refusing to have anything to do with Tony. Gabe's wife, Val, blamed Tony.

Hell. Tony blamed Tony. He was the reason Gabe had become a narc.

Tony drained the last of the beer, then flipped a couple of dollars on the table for a tip.

Time to go home to the little canine.

"WHAT'S HAPPENING?" Andy Wright, the library volunteer, glanced at Dorothy's office after handing Jasmine the small stack of usable books he'd gleaned from the donations pile. Andy didn't talk much, but something was going on behind Dorothy's closed door, and he was as curious about it as was the rest of the staff.

Jasmine shook her head. "No idea, Andy."

He glanced at the door again on his way back to the basement, where the donation books were stored.

"*I* have a good idea of what's happening," Elise, the children's librarian, murmured as she watched him go.

Actually, so did Jasmine. Dorothy had "invited" Chad, the children's library aid, to have a word with her more than twenty minutes ago. It had to have something to do with the dead bolt and the dark form lurking outside the library.

"Why would Chad be breaking into the library? I mean, he's a little left of center, but…"

"A little left of center?" Elise pushed her glasses farther up on her nose. "What about when he went through that kilt-wearing phase? And the camouflage phase? And the piercings?"

"A lot left of center. But why break into the library when he works here?"

And if Chad *had* been breaking into the library, Jasmine *did* want to know why. Because of him, she'd had an evening she would not soon forget, followed by a sleepless night as she tried to figure out how Ghengis had escaped the house while she was gone.

And she still had that awful feeling in the pit of her stomach when she thought about being detained in the alley by the police, and wondered who might know about it—other than Elise, the one person she trusted to know.

Thank goodness her father was several hundred miles to the south, since he would not see the humor in the situation the way Elise had. Years had passed since Jasmine had officially had to answer to him, but even now she took pains to avoid disappointing or displeasing him—unless it was absolutely necessary. It was less stressful on both of them, so she'd become a master of passive resistance—not something she was exactly proud of, but it worked. Living up to the demands of a perfectionist wasn't easy, and the survival strategies she'd developed over the years were now deeply ingrained.

"It's your break time," Elise said.

Jasmine checked the clock and saw that she was actually ten minutes late. "Let me know if any drama occurs."

Less than two minutes later Elise stuck her head into the staff room.

"Drama?" Jasmine said.

"Someone is here for you."

"Not Brenton…" The last thing Jasmine needed was a heavy dose of pompously flirtatious Brenton Elwood going on about his family tree.

"No. This is more of an art-appreciating hunk."

"Sean?" Jasmine felt her spirits rise for the first time in twenty-four hours.

"In the flesh—and it's mighty nice flesh, too."

One corner of Jasmine's mouth lifted. "I've noticed."

Elise shrugged nonchalantly. "Well, I thought I'd mention it, just in case you needed a reminder. And I'll trade you the end of my break for yours."

"Thanks," Jasmine said, checking herself in the mirror before exiting the staff room. "I owe you."

She'd met Sean Nielsen at the university art gallery three weeks earlier, in front of an oversize painting of a grotesque satyr playing a lute. She'd glanced at him, wondering if she was the only one in the rather crowded gallery who found the painting ridiculous, and amazingly, he'd winked at her. She had never been winked at—hadn't even realized that people winked in this day and age, particularly guys who resembled Brad Pitt. On a good day.

"There's a better painting over here," he'd said and, more charmed than she'd wanted to admit, she'd followed him to a smaller abstract and agreed that, yes, it was much better. After that, it had seemed perfectly natural to walk slowly through the exhibit together, commenting on the artwork, then to go for coffee. A few nights after that it was dinner. Followed by another dinner a week later.

They were proceeding slowly by mutual agreement, but the chemistry was there, and every moment she spent with him made Jasmine more and more aware that Sean Nielsen had all the qualities she was seeking in a man and then some. He had a smorgasbord of desirable male attributes. He was educated, well employed, articulate and caring.

And now, as she crossed the tiled lobby to where he waited by the old-fashioned checkout desk, he appeared to be worried. Jasmine's heart beat a little faster. This didn't look good.

Sean smiled as she approached, and, as always, she was struck by how drop-dead handsome he was. She motioned toward the seating area behind him, since it was obvious this wasn't an I-dropped-by-because-I-was-in-the-neighborhood call and she wanted to receive the bad news—whatever it may be—out of earshot of Elise, who was now back behind the desk.

Sean placed a hand at her elbow as they walked the final few steps together, the contact light, yet somehow intimate. He didn't let go when he said, "I hate to do this, but I have to leave town in a few hours. It's a business emergency. I won't be able to make our dinner date tomorrow."

Déjà vu. Only in the past it had been Jasmine's father who had broken dates because of business.

"That's all right," she replied, ignoring a twinge of disappointment as she met his very blue gaze. "There'll be others." And being her father's daughter, she understood these things happened in the business world. She didn't necessarily like it, but she understood.

"I'll make it up to you."

"No, that's okay," Jasmine replied quickly before she realized he was only talking dinner. She didn't like having things made up to her. Something about all those school events missed by a certain distant parent. Years ago she'd decided that a person either showed up for the performance or he didn't—no gifts or substitutions would compensate for it.

She moved aside as she spoke to allow a patron access to the book drop. "Where are you going?"

"New York." Sean moved with her. "Unexpected calamity. I should be gone for just a few days."

She pushed her hair behind her ear with one hand and continued to wear her game face as she said, "Then call me when you get back and we'll see about another dinner."

"I'm glad you understand," he said in a low voice.

"Hey," Jasmine replied with a passable attempt at a smile, "business is business."

And she should know—it was the Storm family motto.

CHAPTER TWO

TONY WASN'T MUCH FOR peace offerings, but he figured an apology was in order—especially since the librarian had not followed through on her threat to file a complaint against him. Yet.

But she'd presented a valid point the night before. He hadn't treated her professionally, and he wanted to make things right. Besides that, he needed a book.

Jasmine was standing near the desk when he entered, talking to a Nordic cover model. And from the body language, it was easy to deduce a mutual interest. Love in the library. How sweet.

Tony went to the computer, found the section he was interested in, then headed back into the stacks. When he approached the desk almost ten minutes later, the two were still talking. Tony put his book on the counter. Miss Storm did not welcome him with her eyes.

"I'll phone you when I get back," the blond guy said. Jasmine smiled, but the smile disappeared as she returned her attention to Tony.

"I came to apologize," Tony said as soon as Thor was out of earshot. He was a bit surprised at how attractive Jasmine was now that she wasn't standing in the dim light of the alley, totally ticked off. She had great eyes, chocolate-brown—and cold as hell.

"Did someone force you?" she inquired with exaggerated politeness.

"No one forced me."

Jasmine scanned the book's bar code, stamped the return slip with a great deal of vigor, closed the cover and handed the book back to him.

"Thanks," he said.

"I hope you put it to good use."

Which, judging from her expression, was a library euphemism for "shove it."

"You realize that policemen are your friends, don't you? Anytime you have a problem, all you have to do is call."

Silence. Tony gave up the act. "I shouldn't have to apologize for doing my job."

"You could do your job with a great deal more professionalism."

"You're right," Tony said bluntly. "And so could you."

He pulled the book off the counter and started for the door.

So much for public relations. Maybe he just wasn't cut out for the more civilized aspects of his chosen profession. Or, the years in the alleys had wrung it out of him.

"THAT WASN'T A VERY polite way to treat a patron," Dorothy said from behind her.

"I'm sorry," Jasmine automatically replied. But she wasn't. Two wrongs might not make a right, but sometimes they felt kind of good. "I don't think he'll be back too often, but I'll make an effort to be polite when he is."

Dorothy peered over Jasmine's arm at the computer screen. "What did he check out, anyway?"

"Model Ships—Fore and Aft." Which had surprised Jasmine. That he was in the library at all surprised her. Tony DeMonte did not have the appearance of a reader.

"A model builder." Dorothy nodded. "It fits."

Jasmine rolled her eyes, but Dorothy didn't notice. Model-ship building fit the man like a size-five ballet slipper. He lacked finesse.

"Was Chad the person who left the basement door unlocked?" Jasmine asked, wanting to change the direction of the conversation and feeling that, due to her deep involvement in the situation, she had a right to know.

"He got kicked out of his parents' house and has been sleeping in the basement on the sick cot for the past two weeks."

"I didn't realize he had a key."

"He shouldn't have a key. He borrowed the emergency master key from my desk drawer. I hadn't realized it was missing."

"Did you…let him go?"

"I'm going to help him rent a room, and, no, I'm not letting him go."

Jasmine gave Dorothy a surprised look.

"He made an error, but he meant no harm. I just wish he would have told me to begin with."

Dorothy bent to retrieve books from the drop box. Jasmine stacked them on the counter as Dorothy handed them to her one by one.

"Why didn't he just lock the dead bolt?" Jasmine asked. "Then no one would have any the wiser."

"He hadn't realized he had to put the key in the lock from the outside to do that. He simply locked from the inside and shut the door. And since he'd been off work the past two days, he had no idea that anyone suspected something was amiss."

Dorothy straightened and pushed salt-and-pepper hair back from her forehead. "But one good thing has come out of this. I'm going to keep a closer eye on the houses in this community." She shook her head. "A suspected drug house near the library. Imagine."

TONY'S DUPLEX MATE MET him at the carport in the center of their silly-looking mirror-image house. The woman was furious.

"He did it again!"

Tony's head was starting to pound.

"Every time you leave, it's the same. Either he howls or he jumps the fence and digs up my bulbs or rips up the shrubbery. You are simply going to have to contain that beast."

The beast in question began howling from the backyard, and then there was the scrape of toenails on cedar and Muttzilla bounded around the edge of the house, his tongue lolling. He skidded to a stop, then made a show of sitting obediently next to Tony. Tony sighed and placed his hand reassuringly on the Great Dane's head.

"I'll pay for the damage."

"You bet you will."

At this rate, his entire paycheck would be gone before it was cut—and it was time for his mother's quarterly condo payment. A colorful expletive played on his tongue, but he bit it back.

"And if it happens again, I'm calling animal control."

Tony nodded and left with Muttzilla.

"You have got to stop this," he said as soon as they were inside the duplex. "Housing is tight in this town. Haven't you heard?"

Muttzilla tilted his head. Tony went to the fridge for a club soda, then sank into his only chair and leaned back. A long day of doing practically nothing could be exhausting. And a long night of the same tended to ease him toward catatonia.

In order to fill his free time after shift, he'd started working on a model ship, but Muttzilla had crunched it in a fit of what the vet called separation anxiety. Tony planned to start again, but would wait until he was in a place where he could leave stuff out without his dog destroying it.

Eating, TV and reading helped fill the after-shift void, but a guy could only eat, watch and read for so long before he had to move, so in desperation, he'd taken up running.

At first it had hurt. A lot. Running at forty-two was not the same as running at twenty-two, or even thirty-two, but getting back into some kind of shape felt good. He'd never been heavy, but his thinness over the past few years had been from stress and living lean. Surprisingly, he found that running helped clear his mind, and it exercised the dog, thus killing two birds with one stone. Now, if it could just pay the bills.

But it wouldn't, so he'd have to do that the old-fashioned way—by going to work and putting in his time— particularly since he had more than himself to think about.

His mom was still recovering from the investment scam her jerk of an ex-boyfriend had conned her into, and Tony would be bailing her out of that mess for quite a while. In fact, he'd be buying most of the condo for which she was now upside-down in her payments, making resale impossible.

In ten years, he figured he'd have that mess dealt with and he'd also have his full thirty years in with the department, making him eligible for retirement with full benefits at the ripe old age of fifty-two. A good age to find another occupation. One in which he didn't have to live so lean all the time or be someone he wasn't.

"Right, Mutt?" he asked the dog.

He was answered with an audible expulsion of gas.

EVEN THOUGH THEY LIVED in the same part of town, Jasmine didn't think it fair that she kept bumping into Tony DeMonte. Why not someone she enjoyed bumping into? Like, say, Sean?

Elise followed Jasmine's gaze across the dimly lit lounge where they'd stopped for an after-movie drink. "Who *is* that?" she asked, lifting her margarita to her lips.

"That's one of the officers from…that night." He sat alone, his strong profile turned toward them as he talked to the bartender. She noticed that though his dark hair wasn't really as long as she remembered, it somehow gave the impression of being unkempt. Must be the curls.

Elise sipped her drink, watching Tony. "He looks tired."

"I think he looks used up."

"Used up?" Elise continued studying the man, who appeared to be unaware.

But Jasmine wondered. She had a feeling he didn't miss much. "Never mind," she said, wrapping her fingers around the stem of her glass as she focused on her friend.

Elise leaned forward, resting her forearms on the

table, her long blond bangs falling into her face. She blew them out of the way. "So what's your read on Andy?"

"He's pretty quiet. Hard to get a read on that." And to Elise's obvious frustration, when Andy did talk, he tended to talk to Jasmine or Chad.

"Yes." Elise considered for a moment. "But still waters run deep."

"Or you hope, anyway."

"We have talked a little."

"Did you trap him in the basement?"

"Do I have to answer that?" Elise asked, pushing her glasses back up to the bridge of her nose.

"You just have."

Elise gave a small sniff. "I found out why he's volunteering at the library." Jasmine raised her eyebrows encouragingly, and Elise continued. "He wasn't very involved in activities or community service back in high school, never dreaming that kind if stuff might be important five or six years down the road. Now he has to show community involvement on his application to Grayson College. Since he likes books, the library seemed the perfect place to volunteer."

"He wants to be a teacher?" An unnecessary question if he was applying to Grayson. It was a private teacher's college, located in a small town fifteen miles from Mondell.

"He started out in architecture, but didn't like the math. He said he preferred to study historical architecture rather than design new stuff. And that's when he realized that teaching history might just fit the bill. His father was a teacher."

Elise with a history teacher…it actually sounded

perfect. "On a scale of one to ten, how interested are you?" Jasmine asked as she stirred her straw through the slush in her glass with her straw.

"Well," Elise said. "When he started a few weeks ago, I thought he was cute, so it was a three or four, but now that we've been talking on and off over the past week…I'd say a six." Elise took another sip of her drink before confessing, "All right. Maybe a seven." Jasmine raised her eyebrows. "And a half."

"I thought so." Jasmine placed both hands on the stem of her glass, glancing over at the cop again, though she wasn't certain why.

"Now…how about you?"

Jasmine brought her attention back at Elise, who was looking at her expectantly. "What do you mean, how about me?"

"How are things going with Sean?"

Jasmine pursed her lips for a second, then smiled. "They're going well."

"It's about time you found someone. I was getting worried."

"I'm choosy. I can't help it," she said.

"Choosiness leads to loneliness, you know." As Elise had pointed out many times in the past. But Jasmine couldn't help it. She did not want to waste time on someone who was obviously not going to fit into her life—like the professional outdoor guide Dorothy had once tried to hook her up with. He was fun and cute, but he had no financial sense and disappeared sometimes for months at a time. And he hadn't understood why Jasmine couldn't just drop everything and go with him.

"Well, in this case choosiness led to Sean." Who did have the potential to fit into her life quite nicely.

"Touché." Elise finished the last of her drink, then checked her watch. "Some of us have to work tomorrow," she said, easing her sweater out from behind her.

"And some of us get to stay home and sleep late."

"Rub it in."

By the time Jasmine arrived at her house, her keys had worked their way to the bottom of her bag. She propped the screen door open with one foot and was digging deep when something warm and furry bumped against her leg, scaring the daylights out of her. She jumped back, letting the screen door slam shut, and then all she could do was stare.

Ghengis Khat. Outside again, when he definitely should have been in.

IT WAS A GOOD THING that Tony had been contemplating leaving, because a few seconds later he had little choice in the matter. The librarian was back and she was agitated.

"I think someone has been in my house." She pushed a few strands of dark brown hair behind her ear, her eyes fixed on his as though daring him to disagree.

"Why?"

"My cat is out and he should be in." His expression must have said more than words, because Jasmine's jaw tightened. "I definitely left him inside and there is no possible way for him to get outside unless someone opens the door."

"Which was of course locked."

"Of course."

"You're positive." Instead of answering, Jasmine

breathed in deeply through her nose. Tony got the message. "You're positive."

He yanked his wallet out of his pocket and dropped bills on the bar. He'd told her policemen were her friends. Now was the time to prove it.

"HAVE YOU CHECKED to see if the doors are locked?" Tony asked several minutes later as they approached the house.

"Of course." Which was one of the reasons she was certain she'd locked them. It had been nerve-racking to approach the house and cautiously test the doorknobs, but she'd found both the front and back doors locked.

"Stay here."

Tony went to the front door and tried it. It didn't budge. He gave her a tight smile and then headed around the house. He appeared a moment later from the other side.

"Let me have your keys."

Jasmine dropped them into his palm. He frowned at the sequined flamingo key fob, as though surprised that she owned something so whimsical, then unerringly picked her house key out of the five she had on the ring.

"Back in a sec."

Ghengis followed him into the house through the open door. She could hear Tony's heavy steps on her squeaky wood floor, growing fainter as he progressed farther into the house. She was really hoping she hadn't left anything embarrassing lying around.

Man and cat came out a few minutes later.

"If someone has been in there, they don't seem to have disturbed anything. You better take a look."

"Did you check the basement?"

Tony smacked himself on the forehead.

"Very funny," Jasmine muttered as she stepped cautiously into her house. It seemed the same. She had no sense of invasion, but then, did people sense those things? She'd always felt she would, but now…nothing. Out of the corner of her eye, she noted that Tony was watching her. He wisely refrained from commenting.

Feeling a lot like Ghengis on the prowl, she went through the house room by room, checking the spots where she kept her valuables, opening her underwear drawer to make certain everything was intact. She'd heard of creeps who stole underwear, but perverts probably didn't get off on her kind of underwear, she decided as she stared down into the drawer containing the neatly folded bits of utilitarian cotton. Well, that was fine, because she didn't buy her underwear to impress perverts. She bought it for comfort. Her only deviations from that rule were her no-panty-line thongs. But they were bunched up in their usual home in the far corner of the drawer.

"Is everything all right?"

"Uh, yes," Jasmine said as she closed the drawer.

"Want to go through the basement with me before I go?"

She nodded. Part of her was anxious to get him out of there and the rest of her didn't want him to leave until she had seen firsthand that there was no one hiding in her house. And even then, she was still dealing with Ghengis's having somehow magically gotten out of a locked house.

Jasmine followed Tony through the kitchen, casually closing her planner before going down the steep wooden stairs. She didn't want Tony to read her to-do lists. Some things were private—like the fact that she actually wrote down, "wash dark clothes," followed by "dry dark clothes." It made her feel as though she was in control of her life, which was none of his business.

The basement was stacked with boxes that Jasmine had yet to unpack during her year and a half in the house. There were also a few pieces of flea-market furniture she was hoping to sand down and paint during the winter, her bicycle, which she meant to use but didn't, and a washer and dryer, compliments of the previous elderly owner's heirs. Other than that, the place was empty—if you didn't count the cobwebs in the corners. She really had to get down here with the dust mop soon.

As far as Jasmine could tell, nothing was out of place. She checked the small bathroom, and the two rooms that had been intended as bedrooms when the house was built, but had never progressed beyond the walled-off stage. Nothing.

"Do you ever use that?" Tony indicated the exit door on the wall opposite the washer and dryer.

"Every now and then."

"If someone got in that way, the dust would be disturbed, and it isn't."

That was a relief, and Jasmine was glad that there was a silver lining to having dust on the floor. She surveyed the basement one last time and then headed for the stairs. She was two steps up when she said, "I have an attic, as well."

"Let's see what's up there."

The attic door was bolted from the outside, so Jasmine knew no one was lurking up there, but she still wanted to be certain that nothing had been disturbed.

It seemed fine, but…she wasn't sure.

"Thank you for coming. I appreciate your thoroughness," she said after Tony had slipped the bolt back into place.

"No problem. Call if you have any trouble."

"Do you mean that?" She was not asking for reassurance. She simply wanted to know if he was sincere.

He flattened his mouth in a way that told her he probably hadn't meant it. "Yeah. Let me give you my cell."

"ONE MORE INCIDENT AND you'll have to move out or get rid of the dog."

"Yes, ma'am," Tony said into the receiver, using his best placate-the-landlady voice. "And I'll put all the bushes back."

He hung up the phone and stared across the room at Muttzilla, who had his chin resting on his crossed front paws, his deep brown eyes on Tony, the man who had rescued him from certain death. The dog had returned the favor.

"Why are you doing this?"

The dog blinked.

"Are you bored? Do you need a playmate? More toys? Just tell me what it'll take to make you stay in the yard and stop terrorizing that tight-ass next door."

The dog blinked again and Tony picked up the remote.

But instead of moving to lie at Tony's feet as he always did when the television was on, Muttzilla stayed right where he was.

Tony regarded the dog, making an effort to relax the muscles in his face. "I won't say I'm not mad, but I'm not holding a grudge, either. Come on."

The dog heaved himself to his feet and padded across the room, his movements graceful for such a large animal, especially considering he'd once been shot in the hind leg. He put his head in Tony's lap and Tony stroked the dog's ears as he flipped through the channels. Muttzilla slowly lowered himself to the carpet, his lips dragging down Tony's pants until his chin finally came to rest on Tony's foot. All was forgiven, but Tony still had to put back his duplex mate's shrubbery the next day. He couldn't afford to get kicked out of this place before his employment contract was up. Because Mondell was a university town, it had a severe shortage of affordable housing during the school year. Emphasis on affordable. Not that the landlords would gouge rent or anything. It was totally reasonable to have a tiny run-down duplex rent for the same price as your average round-trip flight to Australia.

"Tomorrow we'll do things differently," he told the dog. "Nothing personal. I just need to keep a roof over our heads, and you, Bud, need to be more responsible, so…we may have to put you on a chain." It could kill him to do that, but he didn't have any other solution.

CHAPTER THREE

TONY'S CELL PHONE RANG while he was patting dirt around the base of a small lilac bush that he hoped would take root again—or at least fake it until his remaining six weeks were over. He didn't recognize the number, but he answered the call anyway. It was the librarian.

"I hate to bother you," she said after a quick hello, "but I just got home from shopping and it's happened again."

"The cat?"

"Yes."

"And you're positive you left him inside?"

"He was looking at me through the window when I left."

Tony started to rub his hand over his face, but stopped when he felt the grit on his palm, accumulated during his adventure in gardening. "Your cat must have some secret way of getting out."

"Then maybe you could help me find it."

"Fine."

He had nothing better to do. He put Muttzilla in the car and left to solve a mystery that he quite frankly thought was a figment of an overactive imagination.

Tony parked in the shade so Mutt wouldn't fry in the

late-afternoon sun, and then walked the half block to Jasmine's place. She was waiting for him at her gate.

"Did you walk?" she asked in surprise.

"I had to park my dog in the shade."

"Thank you for coming." Her tone was formal, but there was an undertone of stress. She was spooked.

As they approached the house, the big cat stalked around the corner toward them, his ears back, his eyes wary. He was not a happy cat.

Once again the doors were locked. Once again Jasmine handed Tony the key fob with the flamingo fob. He lifted it by one dangly leg as if it were a dead mouse. She didn't smile.

The house was empty, but this time he noticed the basement was devoid of dust. Quite possibly, like himself, Jasmine had way too much time on her hands.

Tony inspected the door frames, looking for signs of jimmying. He checked the windows. The cat followed him, sniffing at his jeans, obviously getting a whiff of Muttzilla and wanting to familiarize himself with a potential invader.

After the inspection, Tony turned to Jasmine and shrugged.

"This is getting weird," she said.

"I have no idea how the cat is getting out. I can't see any opening big enough for him, and I can't see any sign of forced entry." Although why a bad guy would lock up after forcing his way in was another question. If someone broke in, they wouldn't be that careful about breaking out—unless they were just there for the thrill of it.

"Jasmine." She glanced up, apparently surprised at his use of her first name. Well, he refused to call her

Miss Storm, and he had to call her something. "I'm not sure what to tell you here. The cat is obviously out. Your house hasn't been disturbed and no one is in there."

"So…I just go in and pretend nothing happened?"

"You might want to add 'change the locks' to that list in your notebook. In case someone has a key."

Her eyes went wide. "You read my planner?"

"I just noticed the lists." Lots of them. "The planner was lying open."

"That's no—" She broke off and then steered the conversation in a different direction. "Why would someone use a key to let themselves into my house—and then do nothing?"

"Thrills."

He instantly wished he hadn't said it. But it was a possibility. She was a good-looking woman, if you favored the highly organized. She'd even made notations on what color clothing she was going to wash on which night.

"Do you think someone has been in my house?"

"I have no way of—"

"Do you *think* someone has been in my house?"

"No." She did not react—outwardly, anyway. "But I don't want you to take chances, either."

"Fine." She held out her hand for the key fob and he dropped it into her palm. Her fingers closed around the flamingo. "Thank you for doing this. Again. I will get the locks changed."

"Probably a good idea. Or…" *Oh, man, why hadn't he thought of this before?* He tried to sound nonchalant as he said, "You could rent your basement to a cop and his dog."

"You're crazy." The words popped out of her mouth. "It's not even finished."

"All I need is a bed, a minifridge and a microwave."

She stared at him as if he'd suggested that a felon move into the place.

"Why don't you rent a motel room with a kitchenette?"

"Why don't I just flush half my paycheck down the john?"

"I do my laundry down there. You wouldn't have privacy and neither would I."

"For six weeks, I imagine we could work something out."

"Why do you want to rent my basement?" she said.

"Because you have a separate exit and a horrible backyard."

Okay, not exactly horrible, but other than grass and a lone tree, she only had a few scrubby bushes and a poor excuse for a garage.

She pressed two fingers to the bridge of her nose and squeezed her eyes shut. Tony thought he might be making some headway. "Why," she said without opening her eyes, "is a horrible backyard a selling point?"

"My dog…he likes shrubbery. I'd put everything back. In fact, it would be a lot better than before."

Her eyes had snapped open when he'd mentioned putting everything back. She was already shaking her head and it appeared as though she wasn't even aware of the movement.

"Six weeks and your backyard will be better." Although it might spend time looking worse first.

"No."

"You'd feel safer."

"No."

Tony let out a breath. He'd given it a good shot. But

maybe he and the Mutt could hang on to the duplex for another six weeks. Weirder things had happened.

JASMINE SLEPT ON THE sofa with the lights on. Inside and out—something she hadn't done since her babysitting days when she'd watched one too many teen slasher flicks alone. Ghengis slept on her legs, and even though they were numb from his weight in the morning, she appreciated having him there, much more than she would appreciate having Tony DeMonte in her basement. Having him living below her would be more unsettling in many ways than wondering how her cat had mysteriously gotten out twice.

And it annoyed her that he'd said her backyard was horrible. Maybe the grass was about a mile too long, but that was only because her regular mowing kid had moved. And even though the old wooden garage with its gaping door wasn't exactly picturesque…

Well, maybe he had a point.

But saying it, instead of just thinking it, had been impolite—especially when he'd been asking a favor. The guy had no tact whatsoever, and was pretty much the last person she would want to share a residence with.

Still, all that aside, he did smell good. And she had no idea why she'd noticed.

JASMINE DIDN'T FALL ASLEEP until the early hours of the morning, and then, of course, her alarm failed to ring. It was almost nine o'clock when she finally got to work, flustered at being late.

Andy was at the computer, helping Brenton with his genealogy research. *Great.*

Jasmine put her fingers to her lips and tried to sneak into the staff room, but Brenton sensed her presence and turned, his face breaking into what he intended to be a suave smile. His smarmy self-assurance might charm other women—although Jasmine had serious doubts—but it had no effect on her. That did not slow Brenton down one bit. If anything, it made him more determined to impress her.

"Jasmine, when you have a minute, could you offer an opinion on something?" he asked importantly.

"Certainly," she said. "I just have to take care of a few other matters, then I'll be right out. Ten minutes, tops."

He gave a thumbs-up, then turned back to the screen. Chad and Andy joined Jasmine in the staff room a few minutes later, Andy recording his volunteer hours on the chart hanging from the back of the door and Chad popping open a soda as Jasmine finished making arrangements over the phone to meet the locksmith the next afternoon.

"Did you lock yourself out?" Chad asked, after chugging at least half the can and then wiping his mouth with the back of his hand.

"No," Jasmine said. "I'm going to have the locks changed. The ones I have are old-fashioned and sticky, and I'm tired of wrestling with them." It was a reasonable explanation and Jasmine didn't think the world needed to know about her cat problem, especially when she didn't quite understand it herself.

"Is your house older?" Andy asked with interest as he settled his ball cap on his head.

"No, not really," Jasmine said. "There *are* some nice Victorian houses in the neighborhood. Unfortunately, I don't own one. I think my house was built in the 1940s."

Very little work had been done on it over the previous few decades—which was one reason Jasmine had been able to buy the place for a reasonable price. Additionally, and to Jasmine's benefit, the family had been keen to get rid of it as soon as they could after the woman had passed away.

Jasmine looked out the door at Brenton, who was waiting impatiently at the computer. "Who's he related to today?" she asked Andy.

"Everyone except for women he wants to date," Chad interjected before Andy could speak. "So he must not be related to *you*, you lucky girl." He waggled his eyebrows at her.

"He might as well be, for all the good it'll do him," Jasmine said with a clip in her voice. She was tired and cranky and not feeling one bit repentant about it. "And you'd better not let Dorothy catch you taking an early break. Not while you're on her list."

"At least *I* was here on time," Chad said, unabashed.

Jasmine restrained herself from pointing out that he was probably on time because he'd slept in the basement. She knew that ultimately she wouldn't win since Chad spent most of the day thinking of weird things to say. So instead she went out to help Brenton add yet another illustrious relative to his background.

THE ONLY THING THAT saved Jasmine from a serious overdose of Brenton Elwood pomposity was the unexpected sound of her cell phone, which she'd forgotten to shut off per library regulations. She was not having a good day.

Dorothy poked her head out of her office as the phone

buzzed for the third time and Jasmine mouthed an exaggerated, *I'm sorry,* before dashing off to the staff
room. She yanked her purse out from deep within the
staff cupboard, dug for the phone, then automatically
checked the number on the display before pushing the
End button.

It was Sean. Jasmine quickly checked for Dorothy,
who was busy lining out Chad, and then answered the
call.

"Hi," Sean said. "Do you still have this Wednesday
off?"

"Yes." She hoped he'd understand why she was whis-
pering. She worked in a library, after all. He could
probably figure it out.

"I'll be home late Monday. I want to take you out to
dinner on Tuesday."

"It just so happens I'm free." She couldn't help smiling, even as she was keeping an eye out for Dorothy.

"Great. And I *am* bringing you something. But," he
added firmly, "it's not to make up for missing the dinner
date. It's just because I want to."

"In that case, I can't wait to see it."

"Hot date?" Dorothy asked in a stern voice once
Jasmine had returned to the desk.

"Yes," Jasmine confessed.

"Good for you. Now, keep that phone off."

JASMINE LEFT THE LIBRARY that afternoon marveling at
how such a potentially rotten day had turned out so
well. She was looking forward to her date with Sean,
and Brenton had thankfully disappeared while she was
taking the call, so she hadn't had to endure too much of

his self-important flirting. Then, to top things off, Ghengis was sitting on the correct side of the living-room window when she arrived at her house.

She opened the front gate feeling as though a burden had been lifted. Up until last week, her house had been her haven; but now, even though both Tony and her logical brain insisted there had to be an explanation for Ghengis's being outside when he should have been inside, she felt jumpy.

She unlocked the front door and pushed it open, only to have Ghengis shoot out between her legs. "Hey!" she shouted, but the big feline ignored her as he trotted across the lawn toward the low back-fence gate, his favorite escape route when he left the yard to terrorize small dogs. Jasmine dropped her tote and chased after him. Peaches was still out and she didn't want an incident with Mrs. Thorpe, Peaches's owner. The woman was an excellent neighbor—unless her poodle was threatened—and Jasmine truly wanted to retain good neighborly relations.

"Ghengis, don't even think about it."

He feigned innocence, pausing to sniff nonchalantly at the door of the old wooden garage, which was perpetually cracked open due to a bad hinge, and then he disappeared inside.

Trapped. Jasmine heard the distinctive clatter of a rake being knocked over as she approached to capture the cat. She really had to organize the hodgepodge of tools the previous owner had left in there. Either that or hire Chad to do it. Apparently, he could use the money. The big question was—if she did that, could she put up with his irritating ways?

She pulled the door open, crouching to block a feline escape, but instead of a cat, something big, something *huge,* came at her from inside the shed, hitting her hard, knocking her flat onto the grass. She heard a curse as…*it*…tried to jump her body, but it tripped over her legs, landing hard on top of her, knocking most of the wind out of her lungs. Stars exploded as an elbow caught her in the face.

Jasmine struggled to sit up but was knocked down again. She twisted to her belly, dug her fingernails into the ground, trying desperately to break away, only vaguely aware of Ghengis letting out a long growl. And then a streak of gray sailed over her.

Her assailant cried out and rolled off.

The second that she was free, Jasmine scrambled to her feet, gasping for breath and stumbling as she ran toward the front yard, fully expecting the guy to pursue her. She shot a look back over her shoulder in time to see a person wearing a black shirt and jeans vault over her fence and drop down onto the other side into the alley. The sound of running footsteps rapidly faded away.

Pressing a hand to her pounding heart, Jasmine took a few shaky steps forward, still trying to grasp that her cat had saved her. Ghengis, fluffed to double his normal size, crouched near the spot where the intruder had disappeared over the fence, his ears flattened against his skull, his tail twitching fiercely.

"Ghengis?" Jasmine said. The cat peered over his shoulder, and then his ears slowly regained their normal position as he walked back to where she stood. He rubbed his head against her leg reassuringly, then settled at her feet to begin a victory bath.

He'd earned it, but Jasmine cut the bath short, picking him up with both hands and lugging him over to the car. She got both of them safely inside, locked the doors, then used her cell phone to dial 911.

TONY WAS SO CLOSE TO eviction he could smell it. The chain, the toys, the videotape of himself talking…nothing had worked, so in desperation, he brought Muttzilla to work with him. It was an evening shift. The car wouldn't get too hot, but it also wouldn't get any bigger.

When Tony locked the door, the dog was lying across the small rear seat, his nose pressed against one partially opened window, his tail thumping against the other. Tony walked across the parking lot, but glanced back when he reached the side door to the station. The dog was still watching him—either that or he was stuck in that position. Tony entered his code into the key lock and went inside.

He had started down the corridor to his desk, debating as to whether he could slip out for some dog walking on his break, and then did a double take as he passed a waiting area with a young woman sitting in it, an ice pack held to her face.

"Jasmine?" He crossed the space separating them and knelt next to her chair. "What happened?"

Her uncovered eye was swollen, so he could only imagine what the other one looked like.

"It appears I was attacked by a figment of my imagination," she said with justifiable bitterness. Then she swallowed. "I was thinking…maybe we could work out some kind of deal on my basement."

Instead of answering, Tony pulled the ice bag away

from her face, to reveal the beginnings of a lulu of a bruise. He returned the ice pack to the bruise, and then brushed the hair away from the side of her face where it was sticking to her damp skin. He tucked the strands behind her ear, and she shivered, but whether from a flash of memory or his touch, he didn't know.

"Tell me what happened," he said. She swallowed again, then told the story, the words coming slowly in some places, rapidly in others.

When she was done, Tony sat back on his heels, wondering at the sense of outrage coursing through him. He'd seen stuff a million times worse than this, but the thought of Jasmine being knocked around really pissed him off.

"Can I move in tomorrow?" he asked.

"Or tonight after your shift," she said quietly. "I'm almost positive I'll be awake."

CHAPTER FOUR

TONY ARRANGED FOR ONE of his associates to follow Jasmine home and go through the house. After the polite, rather bored-looking officer had given her the all-clear and departed to do more exciting things than walk through a house with a nervous woman, Jasmine paced from room to room with Ghengis at her heels, and double-checked to be sure the officer had not missed anything, then checked again. She was not ready to settle down and face the night alone.

But she was not phoning her father, either. Despite being frightened, she did not need the added stress of her dad somehow twisting things around so that she was to blame. She'd tell him in a few days, when she could do so without sounding upset.

Just one of those things, Dad. I was in the wrong place at the wrong time. So how's the new project going, the one I know nothing about because you never call me?

She couldn't pull that off right now.

If Sean was in town…would she call him?

She wasn't certain. She liked him, but their relationship was still young. Did she want him to see her like this? With her face swollen and her eye black-and-blue? Probably not.

Not yet, anyway.

In the kitchen, Jasmine closed the curtains over the window to the point of overlapping, then returned to the living room and checked the curtains there.

If she kept moving, kept the adrenaline flowing, she could never relax, so she forced herself to sit down on the sofa and face the blank television screen. Ghengis jumped up beside her, and she hauled him onto her lap and hugged him. Surprisingly, he allowed it.

She'd lived in Mondell since college, but other than Elise and Dorothy, she did not have a large circle of friends—at least, not friends she could call and ask to bunk with. Elise was away for the weekend and Dorothy... Dorothy would be annoyed that Jasmine hadn't contacted her, but frankly, Jasmine didn't feel up to Dorothy's ministrations any more than she felt up to deflecting her father's inevitable insinuations that she was somehow to blame. And then there was always the possibility that Dorothy would launch an investigation. Jasmine wasn't ready for that, either.

But according to the police, there was nothing to investigate. Jasmine had simply surprised a man who'd been searching the garage for tools to pawn in order to finance a bag of rock cocaine.

The theory seemed logical from a law enforcement standpoint, but Jasmine wasn't convinced. She'd mentioned to the investigating officer that she thought someone had been in her house recently, and he had visibly perked up—until she added that her only evidence was that her cat had been outside when he should have been in. The guy's expression had frozen and he'd nodded politely, making Jasmine feel more than a little foolish.

The story did sound lame, even to her.

Her eye was beginning to throb, so she eased the Ghengis off her lap and went to the kitchen to make a cold pack out of an ice-filled Ziploc bag and a washcloth. When she returned to the living room, she stretched out on the sofa and eased the ice over her eye. Ghengis once again settled close to her.

Thankfully, the next day was Sunday. She wouldn't have to explain her bruised eye just yet. And then, if she made it through tonight and had a quiet, uneventful Sunday, things would start to feel more normal again. They had to. It was just a matter of time.

Except that Tony DeMonte was moving in. *How normal was that?*

Not normal at all, which was unsettling to a person who organized her life as a hobby. Jasmine hated it when things edged out of her control, and tonight things had more than edged—they had blasted. And she still wasn't quite certain how to handle it.

She rubbed her fingertips over her temples and Ghengis butted his head against her in a comforting kitty caress.

Last week her life had been so blissfully on track, and now, seven short days later, she had a cop about to take residence in her basement and an assailant had been hiding in her garage.

What next?

She was almost afraid to speculate.

JASMINE WAS ASLEEP WHEN the phone rang, bringing her bolt upright, heart pounding. The room seemed abnormally bright, as well it should, since every light was on.

The phone rang twice more before she collected herself enough to pick the receiver up, but she didn't say hello.

"Jasmine? It's Tony." Jasmine's heart rate slowed at the sound of his distinctive voice, deep and reassuring. "Are you all right?"

"I was asleep," she said.

"How are you doing?"

She almost said *fine,* but she wasn't feeling all that fine. So she went with truthful. "Still somewhat shaken." And her eye was throbbing again.

"That's understandable. Is someone with you?"

"No." She looked around for the Ziploc bag, then found it on the floor, now filled with more water than ice.

There was a brief pause, as though Tony was processing the fact that she'd chosen to handle the situation alone. "I'm getting off shift soon. Do you want some company tonight?"

"I, um…" She cleared her throat. "I think I'm doing okay." She didn't particularly want to be alone, but asking a relative stranger to drop in and hold her hand…she wasn't that desperate either.

"Do you still want a tenant?" Tony asked quietly.

An opportunity to change her mind.

"Yes, I still want you to move in." The words emerged on a husky note.

"Then I'll be there in a few hours."

"Right." She pushed her hair back, wincing as she grazed the injured side of her face. "Good night."

"Good night."

The line went dead and Jasmine was once again alone, with the exception of Ghengis, her guardian, who was at the foot of the bed, his front paws folded under his chest. She set the phone on the nightstand, then settled back against the pillows, not bothering with the makeshift ice pack but instead forcing herself to breath deeply to counteract the throbbing.

That something as simple as the phone call had terrified her disturbed her, but what did she expect? An assailant had whomped her in her own backyard. There were bound to be aftereffects.

Jasmine didn't like aftereffects and she didn't like feeling out of control. She wanted things back to normal. Fast. To do that, she had to examine the situation logically, use rationality to dispel her unfounded fear. She had to convince herself the police were right.

Jasmine settled a hand on Ghengis's back and stroked. The big cat leaned into the caress and started to purr, which helped her taut muscles relax. No danger if Ghengis was purring.

So what were the facts?

There had been a man in her garage.

A huge, dark hulk had charged straight at her.

The man had knocked her down and run away.

It had hurt when he'd knocked her down. Stars had exploded.

She'd been afraid he'd continue hurting her. That he'd wanted to hurt her.

If he'd been there to hurt her seriously, he could have done it right then.

Instead he had bolted—which meshed with the police theory that he hadn't been there to hurt her. He'd just been trying to get away.

And then there was Ghengis Khat, who'd been out at least two times when he should have been in.

She had no explanation for that, other than someone had let him out. But why would anyone break into her house and do nothing except for let the cat out?

Thrills.

Tony's words echoed and she shuddered involuntarily at the thought of someone sneaking into her house just for the thrill of it.

She reached out to haul Ghengis up against her chest, ignoring his protesting grumble at losing his comfortable position. Again. His weight felt good in her arms. Reassuring and warm.

Nothing had been disturbed in her house on either occasion she'd found Ghengis outside. Not a thing. She knew that because she'd checked every nook and cranny about two dozen times after Tony had left, just to make sure.

So what did all of this add up to?

Her conclusion was that the police were right. There was no stalker. The man in her garage had been a meth head searching for something to sell in exchange for a bag of dope. No one had been in her house.

She just needed some time to get over the shock of the assault and then her imagination would calm down. And when Tony moved out in six weeks, she'd be ready to solo again.

That was the plan, anyway.

TONY TAPPED ON THE front door very early the next morning. Jasmine was not only awake, but she'd been up for hours, sipping coffee and working out a design for the filet crochet curtains she was making for Dorothy. If she couldn't sleep, she would be productive.

It would help restore that longed-for sense of normality to her life.

She opened the door on the second knock to a tired cop. He couldn't have gotten more than a couple of hours' sleep, but there he was, wearing the faded blue jeans and dark T-shirt that appeared to be his standard off-duty wardrobe.

"I see you made it through the night."

No solicitous concern, but somehow his straightforward comment made Jasmine feel less self-conscious, about her bruise, about having him move in.

"I did," Jasmine agreed solemnly.

"We had patrol cars driving by, you know."

She hadn't, but it made her feel better anyhow. Tony studied her injured eye.

"Colorful, but not as bad as I expected." He tilted his head to see her at a different angle. "Remarkably little swelling."

"Are you an expert?"

"With black eyes? Yes, I am."

"I won't ask for details." Jasmine looked past him to the truck parked at the curb. She saw a mattress and box springs in the back and a giant dog in the cab, almost filling the small space, his eyes fixed on Tony as if he expected the man to disappear at any moment.

"*That's* your dog?" Jasmine was unable to keep a note of shock out of her voice.

"I told you he was big."

"That's not big—that's economy size."

Tony laughed and for one brief moment he appeared younger, almost carefree. Jasmine felt the impact of the unexpected transformation, and then the moment was gone. She blinked. He was surprisingly attractive when he wasn't being condescending or annoying. Not in the same league as Sean, but passable.

"And you're sure about this? Having me move in?" he asked, the laughter fading from his face.

She was pretty certain this would be the last time he'd give her an out. Her last chance to bail.

"I'm sure," she said, before she changed her mind. Now that she was faced with Tony on her doorstep and a truckload of his belongings at the curb, the situation bordered on surreal. She had a man she barely knew moving in. No. She had a police officer moving in, and only for a while—a good deal for both of them. More than that, it was a logical solution.

"I wouldn't want to take advantage of a moment of weakness," he said.

"Funny," Jasmine said without thinking, "but I had the distinct impression you would do exactly that."

A corner of his mouth twitched in acknowledgment, but he didn't smile again. Jasmine nodded toward the truck, where the dog had somehow twisted himself around and was steaming up the back window as he stared out at them.

"Do you want to let him out?"

"In a minute. I'd like to take a look at the room first."

"Are *you* having second thoughts?" Because if he didn't move in, she'd have to resign herself to sleepless nights for a while. Not that she couldn't do it. Her electricity bill might jump, but she could do it.

"Not a one."

She felt remarkably relieved. Even if she could handle things alone, it didn't mean she relished the idea. "Then wait here while I get the keys."

SECOND THOUGHTS? Tony couldn't afford to have second thoughts—not when he'd received official notice to be out of the duplex about half an hour ago. Talk about perfect timing.

Technically, he was supposed to have two weeks to vacate the premises, but the landlady had told him that due to the destructive nature of his dog, she had the right to oust him ASAP, and she was not about to refund a penny of his damage deposit. Or the rest of his month's rent.

He'd argued about the damage deposit, more out of desperation that any hope of changing her mind, pointing out that he had fixed everything as Mutt had destroyed it, but the woman had said she was keeping it on general principle. If he wanted to fight her in court, he was welcome to try.

Tony knew a losing battle when he saw one.

Jasmine was back in a matter of seconds, unaware that her tenant had no way to pay his rent for several days. She led him around the outside of the house to the basement door, the entrance he'd be using, then handed him the key. He unlocked the door, pushed it open, and then together they stepped into the cool interior.

"It needs dusting," she said.

He wondered idly if she was going to write that on one of her lists. "It's fine." Worlds better than some of the places he'd stayed during his undercover stints. Sometimes he'd had decent digs, but for the most part he'd shared grimy quarters with vermin—human and otherwise.

"The bathroom is a little primitive, I'm afraid." She crossed the basement to open the door to the small room. It had a cement floor, with a drain at one end and a showerhead coming out of the cinder-block wall just above it. A canvas curtain dropped from a curved rail to keep the water from splashing onto the small sink and toilet when he showered.

"It's fine," he repeated. *Very much like what you would find in any fine institution.* "I'll feel right at home."

"You'll have to wash dishes in the sink next to the washer and dryer." She gestured to the old appliances that stood against the wall near the door. An antique enamel sink was set into a wooden bench, and above it several pairs of panty hose, two pairs of white panties and a white bra hung from a clothesline.

"I eat takeout," he said, shifting his gaze back to his landlady, the queen of sensible underwear. What a shame. She had a nice shape. And from the slight blush now staining her cheeks, she'd forgotten that her dainties were in plain sight.

"Only takeout?" she asked, thankfully unaware that he was more focused on her underwear than the living arrangements.

"Pretty much."

She nodded as she turned away, probably wondering if she was going to have to arrange an additional trash pickup—or perhaps an ambulance for the coronary he was working on. She walked over to the washer and then turned around. The morning light shining in through the small window above the washer made her dark hair glimmer with threads of red. He never used to notice things like that, and wondered if it meant that he was getting old.

He was feeling old.

Forty-two, and what did he have to show for all those years?

A cosigned condo that he was making payments on

and couldn't live in. A mother he couldn't control but was financing. A job that paid the bills but didn't do much else for him anymore?

Jasmine stayed where she was, leaning back against the washer and regarding him as though she, too, was debating some important issue. Like whether she really wanted him there.

"Is something wrong?" he finally inquired, half-afraid she was going to pull the rug out from under him now that she'd seen Muttzilla in the flesh.

"I'd like to set some ground rules."

Ground rules. No surprises there. In fact, he would have been a little stunned if the list lady *hadn't* set parameters. "Sure," he said in his cooperative voice.

"You'll be here for six weeks, right?" She spoke as if he might move in and then, after six weeks, refuse to move out.

"That's when my job ends."

"If it's not too personal…*why* does your job end? Are you quitting? Transferring?" She absently touched the injured side of her face with her fingertips as she spoke, then seemed to realize what she was doing and dropped her hand back to her side.

Tony didn't mind explaining. If he were a single woman about to let a man move into her basement, he'd want to know a few things about him. "I'm here as an officer on loan. Filling in for an injured officer."

"Where did you work before?"

"Seattle, for the most part."

"For the most part?"

"I worked undercover and had just finished a long assignment on a task force when I managed to finagle this job. Kind of a breather, you know?"

She cocked her head. "You're allowed to *tell* me that you work undercover?" she asked curiously.

"I just did."

"Yes, but…aren't you supposed to have a secret identity or something?"

He laughed. "Not right at the moment."

"Do you do undercover work here? In Mondell?"

He shook his head and she continued with the interrogation.

"If you're on loan, then…do you have another job when this one is over?"

"I'm supposed to." This time he cocked his head. "Now, about the ground rules?"

"No smoking," she said.

"No problem."

"No drinking to excess."

"Define *excess*." He was only half kidding.

She considered for a moment, then said, "More than two drinks a day."

"This'll be like living in a monastery—except… don't they get to drink wine?"

She shrugged but didn't back down.

"Do you drink?" He remembered the frothy umbrella drink she'd had at the bar the night she'd hauled him to her house to investigate how her cat had escaped.

"Not very much."

"But not a teetotaler."

"No. But we're not talking about me. I don't want a drunken tenant."

"Do I have that drunken-tenant look?"

She pursed her lips, as if trying to form a tactful reply.

"Don't answer that," he said.

"Do I have to mention loud music?"

"I'll be a church mouse."

She gave him a yeah-right smirk before pushing off from the washer and started toward the door. He opened it for her and followed her outside into the sun and overgrown grass. Mutt would have a heyday rolling in the stuff. Maybe he would be too busy rolling to eat the bushes.

"Anything else?" he asked as he closed the door behind them.

"If your dog—what's his name, anyway?"

"Mutt," he said, shortening the moniker because he didn't want her to know that he'd given his dog a cutesy name.

"Mutt." She did not seem impressed. "Original."

"Okay, it's really Muttzilla."

She didn't seem any more impressed. "If he digs up my yard—"

"Not if," he warned her. "When. But don't worry— it'll be back to normal when we move out. Better than normal." Which brought him to another point. "This is kind of embarrassing," he said, "but would you be able to wait a few days for the rent?"

She cocked an eyebrow skeptically in spite of her bruised eye, and he plunged on. "It might be a while until I get my damage deposit back from my old place." Like, never. He'd have to juggle a bit to pay his mother's mortgage, plus a new damage deposit and then rent on top of that. "How much is the rent?"

She promptly named a price that made Tony's jaw go

slack. But after he recovered his senses, he fought not to pull her into his arms, swing her in a circle and kiss her, bruised face and all. At that price, he *could* swing the rent in a few days, quarterly condo payment and all. He could eat, too.

"I get paid in four days."

Jasmine looked as if she wanted to ask why a gainfully employed man couldn't come up with a few hundred bucks on short order, but since he didn't want to explain about mothers and scams involving her former lovers, he was glad that she didn't.

"Now I have a favor to ask *you*."

"Shoot."

"I realize the rent is a little low…"

A little low? Try Death Valley.

"Would you mow the yard and do some general repairs while you are here?"

Because his instinct for self-preservation was strong, he managed not to burst out laughing. He cleared his throat and tackled the part of the request that he did have some experience in. "I haven't run a lawn mower in about twenty-five years."

"It's pretty much the same now as it was then," Jasmine replied. "No laser beams or anything fancy. You walk behind the mower and it cuts the grass."

"Sure," Tony said with a shrug.

"And…I'd really like to get that gap in the garage door fixed." She glanced over at the old building, and although she didn't shudder physically, he had a feeling she was shuddering emotionally. "I'd prefer not to have any more surprises. I want it locked shut."

"No problem." Except, he'd never fixed anything.

But he was sure he could figure it out. "You know," he said, curious about why he would cut his own throat and deciding maybe it was because he honestly didn't want to take advantage of her in a vulnerable moment, "I'd do those things regardless of the rent."

"I don't like to owe people."

"I owe you," he said.

"I'd say this is more of a symbiotic relationship."

Which made Tony wonder if his role was that of remora or shark. But he liked the way she was thinking. "Well, I appreciate you renting to us and I promise that we won't bother you. You won't even know we're here."

The words had barely left his mouth when Muttzilla, having somehow squeezed through the partially open truck window, suddenly bounded across the yard after a squirrel, his deep bellowing bark practically rattling the windows.

Jasmine automatically stepped back, her hand pressed to her heart, and Tony sucked in a weary breath. "Much."

CHAPTER FIVE

JASMINE REMOVED THE ice pack and studied her reflection in the mirror. She'd spent a good hour icing the injury, but if anything, the bruise was worse than earlier in the morning. It was actually less tender to the touch, but the purples and yellows were really beginning to show.

She was not going to be ready for that date with Sean in two days.

She brewed a bracing cup of tea before dialing his cell number.

"Hi," she said. "I can't make it Tuesday."

"You can't?"

She was surprised at how reluctant she felt about explaining what had happened, perhaps because she really hated acknowledging it. And then there was the question of how Sean would react. When she'd finally called her father that morning and told him about the man in her garage, first he'd ascertained that she hadn't been hurt, and then he'd wanted an explanation as to why her garage had a sagging door that allowed intruders access, and had she given anyone reason to think that she might have something worth stealing?

Blame Jasmine. That was her father's specialty. But that was her father, not Sean.

"I was involved in…" *What? An assault? A botched burglary?* "An incident yesterday."

"What happened?"

Jasmine blew out a breath. So much for subtlety. "I surprised a man hiding in my garage." Or rather, he had surprised her.

"In *your* garage?" A moment of stunned silence followed, before Sean demanded, "Are you all right? What happened?"

"The police say he was probably looking for things to steal and pawn. He elbowed me in the face as he tried to get away." Jasmine paced the kitchen as she spoke, trying to tamp down the anxiety stirred up by reliving the assault. She grabbed her dishcloth with her free hand and began to wipe already clean surfaces.

"So you're all right?"

"I have a black eye."

"Is that all?"

She twisted around to lean against her stove, bunching the cloth up in her hand. "And a bad case of nerves."

"I'd like to see you."

"I don't think—"

"I used to play football, Jasmine. I've encountered a few bumps and bruises."

"Yes, but to be honest, I'm not wild about the idea of entertaining with a black eye." She resumed polishing with the dishcloth.

"It doesn't *matter* if your eye is black. I want to see you."

"All right," Jasmine said resignedly. "But you've been warned."

"I'll bring dinner, and I'll be there. See you at around seven."

"Dinner? I—"

"Seven."

She pressed her lips together for a moment, said "All right," and then hung up.

She'd find out what Sean Nielsen was made of. If he took one look at her, dropped off dinner and left, at least she'd know she'd been wasting her time.

Damn, but she hoped she hadn't been.

SEAN ARRIVED AT EXACTLY seven o'clock, dapper in his khakis and striped oxford shirt and carrying a wicker basket with a tablecloth folded over the top. His smile froze when he saw her injured eye.

"Oh, wow. Jasmine." He lightly touched her face below the bruise, his expression one of carefully controlled outrage. "I hope they catch the creep."

"You and me both," Jasmine said, stepping back to let him in.

He followed her through the dining room, then placed the basket on the kitchen counter next to the sink.

"Maybe after a glass of wine, you can tell me what happened."

"I'll tell you now," Jasmine said, wanting to get it over with. It didn't take long to recount the story.

"I'm glad you let me come over," Sean said when she'd finished. "The police need to do something about these addicts running amok." He began to pull things out of the basket—a bottle of wine, several foam containers, glasses wrapped in napkins, gold-edged plates.

"I have glasses and plates," Jasmine said.

"I wanted this to be special."

Okay, maybe she didn't have special plates. His were fine china, and the glasses were crystal. Hers were Target specials. Pretty and easily replaced when Genghis, who was now shut in her bedroom, knocked them off the counter.

"Shall we eat in here or in the dining room?"

She gestured at the small table, preferring the more intimate space in the kitchen, and Sean spread the cloth. Irish linen, if she wasn't mistaken.

"What do we get to eat on the special plates?"

"Exactly what I would have ordered if we'd gone out to La Traviata on Tuesday. It's a bit of a shame to have to reheat, but it's better than McDonald's."

"Which was more along the lines of what I'd been expecting," she confessed.

"Really?" He seemed surprised.

"Or maybe a bucket of chicken."

"You'll like this better."

"No doubt," Jasmine said with an ironic smile.

The meal was excellent, the wine was excellent and the company…she couldn't come up with a better description than "excellent." The man was having a detrimental effect on her vocabulary, but Jasmine didn't mind. He knew wine, he had a palate for Italian food and she'd actually forgotten that she had a black eye. The guy was talented.

They were lingering over the last of their wine, the plates pushed aside, when Sean said, "I didn't realize until a few days ago that your father was Richard Storm."

Jasmine felt as though a drip of cold water had just landed on the back of her neck. "How'd you make the connection?" she asked conversationally. Her father was well-known in the business sector, so Sean's discovery shouldn't have surprised her, but somehow it did.

"My company is one of the financial supporters of the economic intern program he set up at Mondell University in conjunction with his business."

Bingo. "Oh."

"It's a good program."

Jasmine smiled but knew the smile didn't reach her eyes. "You still haven't told me how you made the connection."

"During one of the meetings at corporate, mention was made of the plans to honor Richard Storm for his contributions to the College of Economics. Storm is not that common a name and I wondered." He smiled conspiratorially. "Then I did some research."

"You could have asked me."

"Yes. I could have," he admitted. "But I like the investigative process." He tipped his wineglass toward her. "I want you to know, though, that I only investigate people I find…intriguing."

"Oh, yes. We librarians are intriguing," she said as she raised her glass to her lips.

"Now that I'm aware of your background, your career choice does intrigue me. Why libraries? Why not follow in your father's footsteps?"

"I wasn't interested in business. I majored in English lit, and…I like libraries. What can I say? I love my job."

"You're fortunate." He smiled in a way that made her conscious of…possibilities, black eye or not, and then the moment disintegrated as a mournful howl arose from the heat vents behind them.

"What the…?" Sean's shocked gaze met hers.

The howl came again, sad, soulfully eerie. And louder. Much louder.

"It's the dog," Jasmine said, her pulse slowing as she identified the sound.

"Dog? I didn't realize you had a dog."

"He belongs to my renter."

Sean's eyebrows lifted. "I didn't realize you have a renter."

"He just moved in today."

"He?"

Jasmine's spine stiffened at Sean's tone. Her excellent evening was beginning to crumble, but she was not going to explain herself.

"Yes. He."

Sean obviously sensed the shift in her attitude—he'd have to be thick to have missed it. "I wasn't meaning…it's just that your attacker was a man, right?"

"Yes," Jasmine said coolly, thinking he'd come up with a pretty good save.

"How much do you know about your tenant?"

"I know he's not my attacker. He's a police officer."

Sean's expression shifted from suspicious to surprised. "A police officer. Well, I guess that's…trustworthy."

Trustworthy was quite possibly the best word to describe Tony. He wasn't tactful. And granted, he wouldn't have brought china and crystal to a date's house for dinner, but he did seem trustworthy. Plus, he had an earthy sensuality about him that she was becoming increasingly, and disconcertingly, aware of.

"I believe he is, or I wouldn't have asked him to move in."

"Is he a permanent tenant?"

"He'll only be here for six weeks. He's on loan to the Mondell police department and lost the lease on his other place, so I told him he could move in. It seemed like a perfect fix for both of us."

Sean appeared visibly relieved. "He's not from around here, then?"

Another howl. Jasmine waited for it to fade before she said, "No. He's from Seattle and he's returning as soon as this job is over."

"How'd you meet him?"

In an alley during a drug bust?

Jasmine cleared her throat. "I met him at the library."

"I don't suppose *I* could meet him. You know, just so I feel better about the situation?"

"I've been taking care of myself for a long time, Sean." And she wasn't fond of her decisions being questioned and her life monitored. As the old saying went, been there, done that.

"I'm not trying to butt into your life, but this is an unusual circumstance and I want to make sure you're safe."

Okay. She could live with that. "He gets off shift at eleven."

"Maybe we could have coffee on the porch while we wait."

JASMINE WAS SITTING ON the porch swing with the Nordic god from the library when Tony pulled up to the curb. He'd thought about her off and on during the shift, hoped she was doing all right alone. He'd even considered calling her once. Apparently he needn't have concerned himself.

He pushed the car door open and stepped out, mud flaking off his clothing as he moved. The last traffic stop of the evening had not gone as expected, and Tony had ended up chasing the suspect after Yates had tripped and gone down. He discovered he was getting some benefit from his preshift runs. He'd not only been able to catch up to the suspect but had managed to tackle him, as well. Unfortunately, that had happened on the edge of a duck pond.

At least he was almost dry.

"'Evening," he said as he opened the gate.

"Good evening," Jasmine echoed uncertainly.

He knew he didn't look that bad. His hair was dry. He'd wiped most the dirt off, but now, as he stood face-to-face with a guy who'd stepped straight out of a J.Crew catalog, he was wishing he'd changed into his sweats in the locker room at work.

"We had a little trouble with our last arrest."

Thor held out a hand. "I'm Sean Nielsen."

"Tony DeMonte." The guy had a practiced handshake. Not too firm, not too soft. Probably in sales, Tony decided. "Nice meeting you." He released Sean's hand, nodded at Jasmine and then started for the walkway leading to the rear of the house.

Muttzilla let out a long howl and Tony stopped short. When he turned back toward the couple on the porch, he could see from their expressions that this was not the dog's first.

"Has this been going on long?"

"About an hour," J.Crew answered, his voice modulated to express annoyance under the guise of politeness.

Tony ignored him, keeping his attention on Jasmine,

who nodded in agreement. "We're lucky none of the neighbors has complained."

Muttzilla put all his lung power into the next howl and Tony headed for the back of the house.

"Will you be doing something about this in the future?" the boyfriend called after him.

Tony kept walking. He'd deal with Jasmine on this matter. He just hoped she understood that Mutt was anxious and that he would probably calm down with time.

And if he didn't…Tony didn't want to contemplate that. He couldn't afford to get kicked out of another place—especially one he actually could *afford*.

OBVIOUSLY, SEAN WASN'T at all impressed with Jasmine's tenant, but he kept his opinion to himself.

He collected his basket, gently kissed Jasmine goodnight, careful not to touch her bruise, then headed down the walk with a promise to call soon. Jasmine believed that he would. The evening hadn't been a bad one, all things considered.

The dog had quit howling as soon as his owner entered the basement, and her closest neighbor, Mrs. Thorpe, had come home only a few minutes afterward. Before that, the dinner and conversation had been superb.

So why was she feeling…off? As if something just wasn't jibing?

Probably because she wasn't used to evenings ending with her date putting his stamp of approval on her tenant. Definitely an unusual way to end an evening, but a lot of Jasmine's evenings were wrapping up in less traditional ways lately—with the effect of keeping her almost constantly on edge.

Jasmine tidied up the kitchen, then switched off the light and went into her bedroom. She avoided mirrors now, since they now had a tendency to startle her when she saw what she looked like, but since she'd be going to work the next day, she decided to survey the damage after putting on her nightgown. It was, in a word, colorful, but Sean had never given an indication he noticed after his first comment.

Because of her or because of her influential father?

She hated thinking like that. Refused to think like that.

But she'd liked it better when he hadn't known who her dad was—then there had been no question of why he was hanging around.

She shut off the bedroom lights and climbed under the covers just as the basement shower came on, making the old pipes sing. She grimaced at the screeching, but then her lips curved upward as she folded an arm under her head and stared into the darkness.

Having Tony and his dog in the basement wasn't the ideal solution to her situation, but she did feel safer while they were around. And there was a lot to be said for that.

THE BASEMENT WAS COLD, despite the Indian summer that Mondell was experiencing, so after his shower, Tony crawled under the blankets right away. He propped himself up against the wall that served as a headboard before calling his mother. He liked to keep tabs on her to avoid surprises like the one she'd given him earlier that year. Myra was still embarrassed about the fiasco and avoided calling him, so it fell to Tony to keep in touch.

"Hey, Tony."

"How're you doing?"

"Fine." Just enough evasiveness to tell Tony that everything was normal. His mother valued her privacy and Tony had respected that—until she'd lost all that money. "Are you phoning to chat or to check on me?" she asked.

"Both. What are you doing to keep yourself busy?"

"Puzzles. The scanner."

The usual.

"Are you eating?" She'd practically stopped in an attempt to make ends meet before Tony had figured out what was going on.

"Yes, I'm eating. I made friends with a guy down the hall, and sometimes he barbecues and invites me over." She coughed, the result of years of smoking, although she'd quit a year ago. "Any more questions?"

"Do you have enough money until your next check?"

"I'm doing fine."

"I'm only asking because I want you to eat and have some stuff. I'm your kid. This is my job. I'm going to take care of you whether you like it or not."

"Make that a *not.*"

"I hear you, Ma. But don't make this tough on me, okay?"

A long silence followed, and then Myra said, "I know you're taking care of me, Tony. It's just that…I never wanted you to have to do this."

"Yeah. And that's why we're not going to keep hashing this over. If you promise to tell me if you need any more money—ever—I'll leave it alone."

He heard her suck in a long breath, then exhale. "All right. I promise. Now maybe you can just call to talk."

"I can talk now."

"Yeah?" She waited a moment, as though expecting him to renege. When he didn't, she said tentatively, "Well, I heard some things about Lieutenant Brown when I was visiting with the highway patrolman who pulled me over…"

Tony fought a smile as he used his free hand to adjust the pillow behind his head. "Yeah, Ma? What'd you hear?"

"YOU SHOULD HAVE CALLED me," Dorothy said for the third time, her expression one of concern *and* exasperation. Jasmine had arrived at work a half hour early to explain her situation. The bruise was not much better and she didn't want to work the front desk. "I would have come over and stayed with you. Or you could have stayed with me."

"Officer DeMonte was moving into the basement," Jasmine said, "so I wasn't alone. And then Sean visited me last night…I'm sorry I didn't phone you. I didn't want to worry you."

Dorothy had been more than a little surprised when Jasmine had explained that she now had a person renting her basement, but she had not questioned the decision after learning the person was Tony DeMonte.

"You didn't have to come in today, you know. We could have managed without you."

"Thank you, but I want things back to normal." And hanging around the house wouldn't accomplish that.

"Well, I can't say I don't understand." Dorothy handed Jasmine the keys to the outer door so that she could unlock in ten minutes. "I'm sure it was just as the police say, but…I want you to be very aware of your surroundings from now on."

No worries there.

"I promise," Jasmine said solemnly. In many ways, Dorothy was more parental than her own father had been.

"And today we'll have you work in the basement with Chad, finishing the sorting and pricing for the book sale." Dorothy frowned as she studied the bruise. "Are you icing it?"

"Every day, several times a day." Jasmine pulled her sweater off the hook behind the staff-room door. The basement was cold.

"Good. I'll ask Elise to train Andy to run the front desk," Dorothy said as they exited the staff room together.

Jasmine wondered if Dorothy was aware of Elise's interest in Andy. Since she was aware of almost everything, Jasmine had to conclude that Dorothy was playing cupid. Well, good. Maybe this was the boost Elise needed.

"WHOA," ANDY SAID, letting out a low whistle when he saw Jasmine's face. "What happened?"

"Jasmine was attacked in her own backyard by a man hiding in her garage," Elise said, saving Jasmine the trouble of retelling the story for the fourth time that day.

Andy's mouth dropped open. "Attacked! Any idea who it was?"

"No," Jasmine said. "The police think it was someone searching for things to steal and pawn."

"Do they have any leads?" Andy asked, his voice radiating concern.

"No."

"Are you afraid he'll come back?" Chad asked, earning a sharp glance from Elise. "Hey, it's a reasonable question," he said, defending himself.

"I don't have anything worth stealing in the garage. He knows that now." Jasmine spoke matter-of-factly as she tucked two books into the discard box. "Besides, I rented a room in my basement to a police officer, so I'm feeling safer than I might otherwise."

"You're renting your basement?" Chad asked incredulously, his eyes growing round, and Jasmine gave herself a mental kick. *Of all the stupid things to say....*

"It's not a finished basement, Chad. I wouldn't have even considered renting it if he hadn't suggested it."

"*He* suggested it?" Elise asked. "You mean like, 'Hey, you want to rent your basement to me?'"

"Yes. That was pretty much how it happened," Jasmine said, noticing that Andy seemed as shocked as Elise. "You had to be there, I guess. It made sense when he said it." After the attack.

"Wish I'd said it," Chad grumbled, and Jasmine patted his arm.

"Sorry," she said.

"Why does a cop want to rent your basement?" Andy asked with a frown. "I mean, rents are high, but..." His voice trailed off.

"I don't know his personal circumstances," Jasmine said. She didn't want to tell them that Tony was only there temporarily—not with Chad looking as though he wanted to be next in line for the room. She felt bad about Chad's circumstances, and she was willing to have a tenant on a short-term basis until she felt safer, but she was not sharing her home forever—and she was never sharing it with Chad. She'd save up and put in an alarm system first.

CHAPTER SIX

ELISE CAME DOWNSTAIRS just after Jasmine's afternoon break, which she had spent outside, away from prying eyes, soaking up the sun while sitting on the retaining wall next to the basement door.

"Sean's here."

"He is?" Jasmine blinked in surprise.

"Yes, but be warned—Brenton's up there, too."

"Has Brenton asked for me?"

"No. Don't you think that's strange?"

"Yes." Jasmine set aside the box of books she'd been sorting. "Because if the guy in my garage wasn't a meth head, guess who my first suspect would be?"

"I never thought of that." Elise wrinkled her forehead. "And I *can* see him lurking around someone's house."

"I'm sticking with the drug addict theory," Jasmine said as she started up the stairs, "but I need to consider all possibilities."

Sean was in the reading area when Jasmine came upstairs, and Brenton was nowhere in sight. Maybe he'd left.

"They have you working in the dungeon today?" Sean asked.

"So I won't to distract the patrons," she said.

"The bruise isn't that bad."

"Nice try," Jasmine said with a half smile. "Personally, I like the way the purples are graduating into blues and then yellows."

Sean's mouth curved. "Trust me, it does look better, which brings me to why I'm here. Think you'll be up to a public appearance by next Friday?"

"Why?"

"A charity event put on by my company. Dinner. Dancing. An art auction. I thought I'd be out of town for it, but it turns out I won't be. Want to go with me?"

"I'd like that," Jasmine said. If the bruise wasn't gone, she'd invest in some industrial-strength cover-up.

Sean glanced at his watch. "I have a meeting in about fifteen minutes, but I wanted to ask you in person and see how you were feeling. I'll call you later this week with details, all right?"

"All right."

A few seconds later he was leaving the library, and Elise sidled up to Jasmine. "That does it. I'm going to start hanging out in the art museum."

"I thought you had interests here," Jasmine said, doing another quick Brenton check as she spoke.

"I *do,* but I don't necessarily want to put all my eggs in one basket—particularly when I'm not certain that this particular egg is going to hatch."

"The training isn't going well?"

"He seems preoccupied." Elise turned to Jasmine, pushing a hank of blond hair over her shoulder and frowning deeply behind her glasses. "Dealing with an introverted guy is tricky. I don't know if shyness or lack of interest makes him so quiet."

"All I can tell you is that he seems nice."

"Yes. He does," Elise agreed with an expression of determination. "I'll keep chipping away at his tough veneer."

"Good girl," Jasmine said.

"But I may spend a weekend at the museum, too."

JASMINE STOPPED AT THE gate in front of her house. Three days ago she'd faced the exact scene, and had been attacked. But today a giant dog was sleeping under the tree in the backyard, so she doubted anyone was lurking in the bushes or the garage. Not unless they were very gutsy.

She let out the breath she hadn't realized she'd been holding and opened the gate. The dog didn't wake up, but Ghengis blinked at her lazily from the windowsill as she entered the house, before he jumped onto the floor and headed for his food dish. Jasmine felt herself relax.

If Ghengis was hungry, then everything had to be fine.

Or it was until her father called.

"Hi, Dad," she said, wondering if, despite his theory that she wouldn't have been attacked had her garage been in proper repair, he was checking on her. Showing parental concern.

"You are aware that I'll be in Mondell in a few weeks for an awards presentation?"

So much for parental concern. "Do you want to stay here with me?" Jasmine asked politely. She hadn't told him she had a man in her basement. That should make for interesting conversation.

A note of surprise colored his voice as he said, "No. The university is providing me with a suite. I just wanted to make certain you'd be attending the awards dinner."

"Of course."

"Good. It would be embarrassing if you didn't."

"Why wouldn't I?" Jasmine asked, squelching the urge to remind him that *he* was the one who had been absent from events.

"I didn't necessarily think that."

"You're phoning to check," she pointed out.

He cleared his throat. "I need to provide the university with the number of attendees. Will you be bringing a date?"

"I am." Sean. He just didn't know it yet. "His company is involved, though. You may not have to count him."

"His company is involved?"

"That's what he told me."

"What's his name?" There was a rare note of cautious optimism in her father's voice.

"Sean Nielsen."

"I can't place him." But her father would be looking into the matter. Jasmine was sure of it.

"I don't believe you've met."

"Ah. Well, if there's nothing else…"

As in any developments in her case? But she'd downplayed the incident so she couldn't blame her dad for not having asked. She hung up the phone feeling generally depressed. Why couldn't she and her father have a normal father-daughter relationship?

Because it wasn't in her father's character, and she had to accept that once and for all.

"SO HOW'S YOUR LANDLADY?"

Yates found it amusing that Tony had moved into Jasmine's basement after the incident in an alley behind

the library; and, having met Muttzilla, he considered his
partner lucky to have found a home.

"Jumpy." Tony bit into a meatball sandwich, then set
it down to wipe a drip of tomato sauce off his chin. Yates
was poking at a salad.

"Still on the diet?" An unnecessary question, but
Tony had asked anyway, more to redirect his partner's
attention than anything.

"Melanie says I shouldn't have job stress *and* a high-
fat diet. One or the other could give me a heart attack.
Add them together and…" He speared a tomato.

"Easier to change the diet than to argue with the
wife," Tony agreed. But he didn't know if he could live
on lettuce. Yates didn't seem too happy about it, either.

"You've never been married, have you?" Yates asked
without looking up from the greens.

"I came close once."

"What happened?"

I can't be forced to eat lettuce.

Tony bit into his sandwich again, chewed and swallowed before he answered. "She didn't like the way I
disappeared all the time." Undercover work, even
short jobs, didn't lend itself well to relationships.
Some of the guys he worked with had wives who tol-
erated it, and others didn't. His girlfriend, Val, hadn't
been a fan, so she'd married Gabe, who'd then
promptly joined the narcotics squad—mainly because
Tony had pushed him to do so. Tony had been so
enamored of his new job, and Gabe had been such a
natural. Damn, had he known how things would turn
out… He squelched the thought because it ate at his
gut whenever he didn't.

Val had been unhappy at her new husband's career change, but Tony had to give her credit for sticking with Gabe—literally through good times and bad. It was more than she had done with him.

Yates nodded, as though he'd gotten the answer he'd been expecting.

"There was other stuff, too."

"Like what?"

"Like I'm no prize," Tony said with a half smile.

Yates gave a snort that was probably supposed to be a laugh, but Tony had the feeling his partner didn't feel much like laughing.

They continued to eat, Yates spearing at the greens with an uncalled-for vengeance.

"Still pissed about the burglar?" Tony finally asked in his most diplomatic tone, since a guy eating lettuce could turn mean in a heartbeat. Especially one who'd had a rough first half of his shift.

Before they'd hooked up for dinner break, Yates had had two burglary calls, one right after the other—both probably the same ballsy individual, from the looks of things. Yates had arrived too late to do anything about the first one, and on the second one, he'd practically caught the kid in the act, but had been easily outdistanced when he'd tried to chase him down—in spite of the fact that the kid was carrying a bag of loot.

Yates dropped the fork into the salad and pushed the bowl aside. "No. I ran into our friendly neighborhood dope dealer, Robert Davenport, at the beginning of shift. He was real…smug, I guess."

"Forget it," Tony said. "The guy is scum."

Yates leveled a speaking look across the table. "He's

laughing at me because I got that warrant for the house by the library and then couldn't find anything."

"That's what scum does."

"He knows we busted librarians."

"Can't do much about that. We did."

"I want the last laugh."

"It'll happen," Tony said, even though he'd been in law enforcement long enough to realize that it might not. Some guys were hard to stop. Davenport would probably screw up at some point, but until then…well, Yates would have to live with it.

Hopefully, he wouldn't get an ulcer in the process.

JASMINE DIDN'T HAVE a right to go into Tony's room, but she had to make sure the small window was latched before she went to bed. She pushed open the door. With just a glance she could see that the window was secure, but once she was there, she took a moment to study her surroundings.

Tony DeMonte lived a spartan existence. No. *Spartan* was a generous description. Everything was stashed under the twin bed. His boots were set side by side close to the wall. The bed was neatly made, with hospital corners. Jasmine had somehow expected more disorder from a guy like Tony.

She eased the door shut, then headed for the stairs, noting the small changes that had occurred since Tony had moved in. His toothbrush and toothpaste were perched on the edge of the old-fashioned laundry sink. A jumbo bag of dog food leaned next to the wall near the door and a jumbo dog lay on the doorstep outside, waiting for his man to arrive home.

The room smelled of spicy soap, or maybe after-shave, that made her senses tingle. She did her best to ignore the sensation, which she shouldn't be having in the first place.

Things were different now that Tony'd moved in. She still felt a touch self-conscious having someone else in her house, and wondered how she would feel after he left in a matter of weeks. Relieved? Or still nervous about being alone?

She slowly went back upstairs, leaving the spicy scent behind.

TONY GOT HOME FEELING tired and pissed after his first afternoon shift.

Since he and Yates had talked over lunch a few days earlier, more burglaries had occurred, and now his ribs were aching from hitting a garbage can while trying to chase down a guy who'd been hanging in the alley behind an electronics store.

And he was concerned about Yates, who seemed to be growing obsessed with the idea of taking down Robert Davenport, when leaving the guy alone and letting narcotics take care of things was probably saner. He'd have to have a talk with him.

All in all, he was not in the best of moods, but did his best to suck it up when Jasmine stepped out onto the front porch as soon as Tony opened the gate, her face strained. The bruise around her eye had faded to more of a purplish shadow, which emphasized her anxious expression.

"Is everything okay?"

"I can't find Ghengis."

Déjà vu. "Did you leave him inside?" *Only to later find him outside?*

He didn't want to deal with this again. He'd tried not to sound sarcastic. Judging by Jasmine's reaction, apparently he'd failed.

"No," she snapped. "I let him outside and he hasn't returned. My point is that you may want to keep your dog inside tonight."

Mutt usually slept outside at the top of the basement stairs, guarding the house from marauders. As long as Tony was inside, the dog was fine outside, and Tony liked the arrangement because Mutt had a tendency to snore. Loudly.

"Why?" Tony asked.

"Because Ghengis has a thing for dogs."

"A thing?"

"He attacks the poodle next door when Mrs. Thorpe lets him out to do his duty at night, and there have been other incidents around the neighborhood, as well. They've all happened after dark."

Tony started to laugh. He couldn't help it. "You think…" He shook his head. "Your cat is not going to hurt my dog."

"He put that man in the garage over the fence."

Tony had heard the story, but he didn't believe it. "Mutt can take care of himself."

"I'm warning you," Jasmine said. She was so serious that Tony wanted to smile. He was smart enough not to.

"Warning received," Tony responded as he started on around the house.

And disregarded.

TONY WAS ALMOST ASLEEP when the phone rang.

"Hi…I hope you weren't nodding off."

No mistaking the husky voice. "Hi, Val. How's Gabe?" He rolled over onto his back, rubbed a hand across his eyes.

"He went into rehab today."

"For real?"

"I hope."

She always did this—called to let him know Gabe's status, usually late at night—but it wasn't so much to keep him informed as to trip the guilt trap. And he had a feeling that she wouldn't have minded if he chose to drive through the night, because of that guilt, and make things all better for her.

"How long?"

"No telling." Her voice got even huskier, in the way that had once driven him so crazy. "When are you coming back to Seattle?"

"Not sure." Tony pushed his hand over his face again. "Listen, Val. Things'll pick up once Gabe's out. This'll be the hardest part—for both of you."

"Right." Her voice was less throaty now that she wasn't getting what she wanted. "I just thought I'd let you know."

"Thanks, Val."

She hung up before the last word was out of his mouth.

For him to fall asleep again took forever, so Tony's mood bordered on ugly when he was roused up out of slumber by the sound of… He didn't know what, but whatever it was, it was getting the living daylights beat out of it.

After a few seconds, he realized his dog was making that horrendous noise.

Tony jumped out of bed, stopping just long enough

to yank his boxers on before jerking the door open and stepping out into the muggy night. He had to get Mutt shut up before one of the neighbors called the cops. Not that he couldn't talk his way out of it—he just didn't want to deal with the crap they'd flip him tomorrow.

"Mutt!" He didn't bother trying to keep his voice down. Everyone within a two-block radius had probably been awoken by the cacophony. Muttzilla appeared out of the darkness, heading straight for the basement door at top speed.

"Whoa…" Tony sidestepped Mutt, who slid to a stop, barely avoiding tumbling down the basement steps. A second later, Jasmine's giant cat launched himself from out of nowhere, straight onto the dog's back and the fight was on. Again.

Tony looked around for the hose—for something, anything, he could use to separate the animals. He wasn't going to use his hands, that was for sure, since he was fond of them and wanted to have them in the future.

The back door opened. "What…?"

But Tony already had the hose. "Turn on the water."

"What?" Jasmine had lapsed into a single-word vocabulary.

"Turn on the—"

A split second later water shot out of the hose and Tony sprayed the flailing bundle of fur, teeth and paws in front of him.

The water had no effect on Mutt, but Genghis suddenly realized he was getting soaked. The animal gave a bloodcurdling screech, then flew off into the night.

The water trickled to a stop and Tony dropped the hose. Mutt started rubbing his nose with his paw.

"Over here, big guy. Let's look at you." He grabbed the dog's collar and led him toward the porch light, where Jasmine stood in her robe. Muttzilla whimpered.

"Is he hurt?"

Tony checked the dog's eyes, but they seemed fine. "Just scratched up."

"I want you to know I've called the police!" a masculine voice shouted from out of the darkness.

"Thank you," Tony called back just before a distant door slammed. He glanced up at Jasmine and could almost hear her grinding her teeth.

"Maybe he should sleep *inside* from now on."

Tony was in no position to argue, so he said, "Right."

"Do you have anything to put on his nose?"

A big drop of blood was forming on the tip, with several smaller beads close to it.

"No."

"Wait here."

Yeah, like he was going to follow her inside when she was in this kind of a mood. He wondered if she knew that the porch light made her robe see-through.

She appeared a minute or two later with a tube of animal ointment and silently handed it to him. A car pulled up in front of the house. Tony handed Jasmine back the tube. "If you handle the blood, I'll handle the cops."

"In your boxer shorts?"

Tony glanced down, then thought, *Screw it,* and headed around the house to meet his brother in blue. The sooner the patrol car was out of here, the sooner he could deal with Jasmine.

Several minutes later Davis drove away, laughing, and Tony returned to the backyard to face one angry landlady.

"I'm sorry I left the dog outside," he said, hoping to block her attack. "You were right. Your cat is vicious."

There was no question in his mind which animal had instigated the attack, since Muttzilla had never shown aggressive tendencies toward another living thing, except for certain species of the plant kingdom and a drug dealer who'd kicked him one too many times.

"I would appreciate it if, when you left the premises, you wore *pants.*"

"I think Officer Davis has seen boxers before."

"But I'm not so sure about my *neighbors.*" She spoke through clenched teeth. "And now they have seen *you* standing in front of *my* house in the middle of the night, in your underwear and not a whole lot more!"

Tony rubbed a hand over his forehead. "For all they know these are regular shorts."

"I cannot believe I'm having this argument. Wear pants."

And with that, Jasmine stalked into the house and shut the door. Hard.

"Come on, Mutt. I think you'll be spending your nights inside for a while."

CHAPTER SEVEN

YATES PULLED INTO THE courthouse parking lot, next to Tony's car, a few minutes before the shift began. Obviously preoccupied, he made an effort to clear his features when he saw Tony.

"Everything okay?" Tony asked.

"Yeah." Yates's clipped tone belied his answer.

"You haven't had another run-in with Drug Dealer Davenport, have you?"

"No."

Tony gave a grunt of understanding, even though he had no idea what he was understanding, as the two walked into the station prior to another long shift.

"Hey, thanks for the technical advice." Following Yates's over-the-phone instructions, Tony had attempted to make amends with Jasmine by fixing the sagging garage door, which was now amazingly back up on its hinge and padlocked shut.

And he knew being amused was wrong, since he'd been the one at fault, but he couldn't help smiling every time he recalled what had happened the night before. Jasmine had been so flaming mad. There was more to the librarian than she let on—and Tony kind of felt like getting her dander up again, just to see what would happen.

"Glad to help," Yates said, bringing Tony's thoughts back to the present. "So it went okay?"

"Yeah. Once I found tools, that is." For a guy who'd only handled a gun and a cue stick, he thought he'd done a decent job of reinforcing the broken wood on the door with an old piece of fencing and screwing the hinge back into it.

In fact, doing something that didn't involve throwing some scumbag down on the ground felt good. He might have to do more of it in the future.

MUTTZILLA HAD GOTTEN his revenge for the Ghengis attack by digging at least a dozen big holes in between the time Tony left for work and the time Jasmine returned home.

She stood for a long moment at the gate, gaping at the minefield that had once been her yard, remembering what Tony had said about putting everything back.

"You can bet your sweet behind you'll put it back," she muttered as she closed the gate and walked to the rear of the house, surveying the damage as she went. And it irked her that last night she'd noticed that Tony *did* have a nice behind. And legs. His chest wasn't bad, either.

She was not the kind to be attracted to rough-edged men—and a guy like Tony did *not* fit into the vision she had of her life—so she was ticked that she found him attractive, even if on a very primitive level. Especially after the trouble he'd caused by ignoring her warning and letting the dog sleep outside.

She cast a quick look at the old garage as she rounded the back of the house, and then her jaw dropped. The garage door had been repaired. And padlocked shut.

Tony had repaired it for her, which made it harder to stay annoyed at him, even though annoyed felt a whole lot more comfortable than grateful. She refocused on annoyed as she continued into the backyard, expecting to see further mayhem, but the scrawny bushes had not been touched. It had apparently been a digging day.

The excavating culprit was lying under the tree, his sad eyes on her as she halted in front of him, hands on her hips. He knew he'd been a bad dog, and Jasmine couldn't bring herself to chastise him. The big guy was obviously dealing with issues. Kind of like she sensed his owner was.

But cops tended to have issues because of the people they were and the life choices they had made. Dogs… dogs had issues thrust upon them, and she felt sorry for Muttzilla.

She knelt and held out her hand for him to sniff. He turned his head away. "It's all right," Jasmine murmured as she got to her feet.

To her surprise, the dog also got up, and followed her. She scratched his ears when they reached the back step, and was rewarded with a tongue-lolling dog grin.

"I can't let you in," she told him as he trailed up the steps. "Not after what happened last night."

She actually would have liked the big dog's company for a little while, and she sensed he would have happily provided it, but she couldn't risk a repeat of the battle royale in her living room.

Not without Tony on the other end of the hose.

TONY HAD NEVER BEEN a big fan of quiet patrol shifts. Early in his career he'd found that monotony made him complacent, which was hazardous to his health. That was one of the reasons he'd worked his way out of patrol and into a position on the narc squad. He liked the novelty of assuming a role, seeing what happened. He was quick on his feet, and since he really didn't have much of a life outside of work, he hadn't minded when the role took control.

He was no longer willing to let his work rule life, and the novelty of undercover assignments had long since worn off, but that hadn't made him any more enamored of quiet patrols.

Yates didn't seem to mind the boredom that drove Tony so crazy. If anything, he embraced it, and Tony was beginning to think it was because of his wife, Melanie, and the fact that she wasn't wild about his job. He could go home and truthfully tell her that he'd had a quiet routine patrol.

Today was going to be ultraquiet, since he and Tony had both spoken at a chamber of commerce luncheon—Tony had given tips on how to spot a meth lab and Yates had elaborated on crimes conducted out of hotel rooms. They'd managed to throw in a warning about the rash of burglaries, but most of the store owners in town were aware and taking precautions. On the way back from the luncheon Yates drove, but he didn't have much to say. It was becoming the norm of late.

Tony hated to butt into Yates's business, but he did anyway, asking if everything was all right.

"Yeah. Except that I keep running into Davenport. And he smiles at me."

"You gotta ignore it."

"Yeah. But he's so smug I'd just like to belt him, you

know?" An ancient sedan cut him off just as he spoke. He cursed and a few seconds later pulled the barge over.

Tony met Yates's eyes from the opposite side of the car as the jittery young woman handed over her driver's license and tattered registration. He'd seen women like her a hundred times—trying to smile but only able to hold it for a few seconds before she started twitching. A toddler was sitting unrestrained in the rear seat.

"I'll have to ticket you for not having the child in a safety seat," Yates informed her.

"I got one. It's at home. This was an emergency trip to the store." She pushed her hair behind her ear, rubbed her face.

Yates peered into the cluttered interior of the sedan. "What did you buy? Or is it in the trunk?"

"We're going to the store now."

"To buy…?"

"Baby food?" She matched his tone, letting her impatience show.

"Mind if we look inside the vehicle?"

"Nope." She got out of the car and Yates opened the back door so that she could lift her baby out. Yates gave the car a thorough search while Tony watched the mother and kid. The kid kept reaching for him over the mother's shoulder.

"This your pipe?" Yates asked, holding up a glass tube.

"I don't know what that is. I loaned my car out to a friend of my husband."

"Well, in that case…" The baby reached for Yates, nearly toppling out of the mother's hold, and he took advantage of the movement to lift the little boy out of her arms.

"Cute kid," he said, patting the kid's bottom through the thick diaper. He nodded at Tony, who pulled the diaper out a few inches and reached in with two fingers to extract a Ziploc bag.

"How can you do this to your child?" Yates asked, cuddling the kid. The little guy clutched at his earbud.

The woman's mouth pressed into a flat line and then she shifted her gaze to stare in the opposite direction as Tony put the handcuffs on her and told her she was under arrest.

"I asked you a question," Yates said. "How can you do this to your kid?"

"I didn't do anything."

"There's rock cocaine down your child's pants and you didn't do anything?"

"I didn't put it there."

"I'll call child protective services," Tony said. He walked the woman to the car, put her in the back. Yates was still cradling the child, fuming. Yates hadn't experienced quite as much of this as Tony had, and he was taking it personally.

"Kid doesn't have a chance," Yates said after they'd transported the mother-of-the-year to jail and transferred the child to a social worker.

"Probably not," Tony agreed as Yates sat down at his desk, ready to tap out his report. He wished it weren't true, but it probably was. He'd witnessed a lot of kids in rotten circumstances because of their parents' habits. People with dope habits didn't seem to be all that careful with birth control. He went to his own borrowed desk, flipped through a stack of papers on the corner, searching for a report he had to review before court the next day.

"Melanie wants a kid."

Tony stilled at the bald statement, then glanced casually over his shoulder, knowing that if he acted too concerned, Yates would probably clam up. "That a fact."

"But she's afraid she'll be raising it alone."

And there it was—the biggest reason for Yates's preoccupation.

Tony wished he had words of wisdom, but the sad truth of the matter was that he didn't. Melanie had a legitimate concern and there was no use pretending she didn't. Last Tony had heard, law enforcement was a potentially dangerous career.

"She'll come around," he said anyway, refocusing on the papers.

"I hope." Yates got to his feet and pushed his metal chair back across the tiles with a screech, then went to pour himself a thick cup of coffee from the pot at the rear of the squad room. "I'm trying to do the right thing, you know? Go out and do things with her and stuff." He suddenly paused with the coffeepot poised in midair and looked at Tony as if he had just flashed on a brilliant idea he wasn't ready to share. Tony shifted his weight. His warning instincts were activating.

"Hey, uh, speaking of doing stuff together, are you busy this weekend?" He casually put the pot back on the burner to fry some more.

"Why would you ask?" Tony inquired with exaggerated politeness as he momentarily abandoned his search.

"Because I think you should go bowling with Melanie and me."

"Bowling?"

"Yeah. And maybe we could catch a bite afterward."

"Maybe," Tony said cautiously, not liking Yates's overly nonchalant tone. "Does this involve a single sister?"

"Cousin. Melanie's cousin."

"I'm busy."

"Listen, it would only be the one time, and it would get Melanie to stop asking me to find some nice guy for Georgia."

"Georgia? Like the state?"

"I didn't name her," Yates said in a clipped voice. "It'd help me out."

"I don't do blind dates."

"Think about it."

"I'll think about it, but the answer is still no."

JASMINE WAS MAKING SOME progress in her recovery from the assault, although she still hated to arrive home when Tony wasn't there. Her bruised eye had healed to the point that she could hide the discoloration with concealer, and her life seemed to be edging nicely back to normal.

She was, in fact, congratulating herself on the return to routine after a particularly tedious day at work, when Ghengis met her at the gate, looking decidedly unsettled. She'd been in a hurry that morning, and couldn't remember if she'd left him inside or out, but was really hoping she'd left him out, since that's where he was now.

"Have you been fighting?" She leaned down to stroke him and he growled before aiming a bite in her general direction. She yanked her hand out of range. The last time—the *only* other time—he'd done that was more than a year ago, when he'd encountered a dog who'd proved to be almost as tough as he was.

"Are you okay?" she asked, kneeling on the sidewalk next to the cat and taking a chance by lightly running a hand over the top of his fur, not making contact with his body. He growled again and moved away stiffly.

Jasmine stood and regarded the cat, who then sat and began a serious bath, his ears folded back. She didn't see any broken skin or blood. It didn't seem to be a veterinarian matter, but Ghengis had definitely been in a fight. She wondered what kind of shape the other combatant was in and, out of habit, checked the answering machine as soon as she went into the house. No blinking light.

"You're grounded," she said. "For your own good. I'm buying stock in the kitty litter company and you are never going outside again. Get used to it."

JASMINE ATE A QUICK dinner and then, after finding a television show she actually felt like watching, went to her spare bedroom, where she kept her stash of crochet supplies. One more ball of thread and she'd have the first curtain panel done. She could get it finished tonight.

She snapped on the light, took two steps into the room, then stopped and stared.

The cover plate to the electrical socket next to her worktable was hanging askew, the center screw barely holding it in place.

Jasmine forced herself to think rather than react.

It was just a loose cover plate. No big deal.

Except that it was loose on the same night that her cat showed up injured…

No. To find the two related was ridiculous. The screw had probably been stripped since she'd purchased the house. Ghengis had bumped against the unsecured plate and knocked it askew. Or she had hit it herself and hadn't noticed.

A shiver traveled through her body in spite of her logic. She backed out of the room and shut the door, a little ashamed of herself.

She had to go with logic. This was nothing, because…well, what could it be? Some nut who liked to unscrew cover plates? Why on earth would someone be messing with her electrical sockets? It made no sense at all.

But an hour later the situation still bothered her—primarily because of Ghengis. What if he hadn't been in a fight? What if someone had kicked him? Her life, which had been easing toward normal, seemed to have jerked back out of control and she hated it, so when Tony knocked on her door and presented her with the rent, she pulled the door open wide.

"Would you mind giving me an opinion?"

He shrugged. "Sure. Why not."

TONY STEPPED INTO JASMINE'S living room, wondering what had happened now. She was obviously frightened, and trying hard not to show it.

"First of all," she said briskly as she led the way down her hall, "when I got home, Ghengis was upset and I discovered that he was injured."

"Injured?"

"Yes. Bruised."

"How do you think that happened?"

"Well, I thought he'd been in a fight until I saw…well, follow me."

Tony followed Jasmine into a spare bedroom, trying not to notice the nice way she moved—or to at least not focus on it. She stopped just inside the door and pointed across the room. It wasn't hard to see what she was pointing at. The cover plate to the electrical socket was about to fall off.

She moistened her lips. "I'm in here often, and until today, the plate has always been right where it belonged."

A crooked cover plate. Man, what next?

But she'd been assaulted and was entitled to some post-traumatic stress. Besides that, he'd decided the night of the cat attack that he honestly liked her, neuroses and all, so Tony decided to play nice.

He crouched next to the cover and frowned. It was just a plate cover and he couldn't think of any nefarious reason for it to be loose. Unless— He recalled a case where a man had broken into a female neighbor's house and installed cameras so that he could observe her. Unlikely that this would be a similar situation, but Tony had worked in law enforcement long enough to know that anything was possible. People were strange.

"You don't think this means anything, do you?" Jasmine said.

"Honestly? I think Ghengis got into a fight and the plate got knocked crooked somehow. You want to get a screwdriver?"

"I can put the plate back myself," she said coldly, obviously not happy with his analysis.

"I thought I might just check behind it. Just in case."

Jasmine went without another word. She returned a few seconds later with a screwdriver and a flashlight. Tony removed the cover plate and laid it aside. Jasmine knelt next to him. A fresh scent hit his nostrils, stirred an old memory.

Lilacs, maybe?

Whatever it was, it smelled good and made him feel like leaning closer to her. Which would probably make her pop him one.

As far as Tony could tell, there was nothing unusual about the interior of the electrical box. No foreign wires or big fingerprints. He shone the light in the narrow space between the box and the wall. Nothing.

Jasmine sat back on her heels. She wore a stubborn expression, but she didn't say anything.

"Any chance you might have bumped the plate with the vacuum cleaner or something?"

"Of course it's possible."

"I can't think of any reason that someone would be messing with your electrical outlets."

"It does sound crazy," she admitted grudgingly.

"You're bound to be hypersensitive after being attacked."

She met his eyes and he knew they were both thinking about the times *before* she'd been attacked, when she'd had him check the house because she *knew* someone had been there.

"Okay, let me ask you a few questions."

She pulled a breath in through her nose, then nodded.

"Is it possible that your cat was hurt in a fight? Was he out last night?"

"Yes."

"Other than this cover, have you noticed anything else out of place?"

Jasmine glanced away, showing him her unhappy profile as she said shortly, "No."

"Is anything out of place?"

"I'm…not sure." She wrapped her arms around her waist.

"Do you have any indication, other than this plate cover and a bruised cat, that anything is out of the ordinary?"

"Just my gut instinct." Jasmine reached for the screw-driver and flashlight.

Tony hated what he was doing, but he did not believe there was any connection between the big cat, the man in the garage and the loose cover plate. If someone was stalking Jasmine and getting into her house, he was doing it just as easily after she'd changed the locks as before. And he was doing it after Tony had moved in. It didn't make sense.

"Look—"

"I am not a crazy cat lady, imagining things."

"Jasmine—"

"Thanks for the opinion."

Tony gave up. "I'm sorry it's not the one you wanted. Can I go through the kitchen to get downstairs?"

"Yes."

She walked with him as far as the basement door, and he heard the latch slide shut as soon as the door closed behind him.

AFTER JASMINE LEFT FOR work the next morning, Tony went back up the basement steps and checked the latch. She'd put in a load of laundry that morning and had left the door unlocked.

Accidentally or on purpose?

It didn't matter.

He walked through her house, figuring that she'd forgive him, since he was only trying to help.

So why would someone enter Jasmine's house and do…nothing, except for maybe unscrew a cover plate? Was the person looking for something or hiding something? Bugging the place? If so, there were easier and more effective places to conceal a bug than behind an electrical cover in a spare bedroom.

He went up into the attic to check around. The place was dust free, so he couldn't see if anyone had been up here, but if someone had attempted to hide cameras up here, the solid wood floor would have stopped them. The attic was an honest-to-goodness old-fashioned one that kids would love to play in.

Or did kids even do that kind of thing anymore? Maybe they spent all their time plugged into video games. He'd most likely never know, since his biological clock had undoubtedly already ticked past the fatherhood stage. That was fine with him. He hadn't exactly had a stellar childhood.

He headed back down the steps and found himself face-to-face with the giant cat, who was sitting on the counter, staring at him with an evil expression.

"Back off," Tony growled. "And keep your mouth shut about this."

He went down the basement stairs, remembering a time, not all that long ago, when he hadn't talked to animals at all.

"JUST A MINUTE!"

Jasmine froze, her hand on the doorknob, before

turning to her neighbor, who was obviously upset. *Oh, dear heavens. What now?* Mrs. Thorpe only acted this way when her beloved poodle was threatened, but Ghengis was in the house.

"I want to talk to you," Mrs. Thorpe said, stating the obvious. "Do you have a license for that, that…*dog?*" she asked, wagging a finger over the chest-high fence at Muttzilla, who lay under the tree between two craters, his chin on his paws.

"He's not mine," Jasmine said.

"Then he belongs to that man you're living with?"
That man you're living with.

Jasmine felt both an impulse to set Mrs. Thorpe straight and a twinge of contrariness that made her want to keep quiet. She kept quiet. There was no reason for her neighbors to know her private business. Maybe, despite her father's stern tutelage while growing up, she didn't care what people thought.

"Do you have a problem with the dog?" Jasmine inquired respectfully. She'd never seen Mrs. Thorpe so steamed, even after Ghengis had chased Peaches around her yard a few months back.

"Just take a look here and then ask me that question." Jasmine walked to the fence and peered over.

Muttzilla had been busy that day.

"He terrorized poor Peaches, which I'm sure you know. I got back from my club meeting and there that monster was, in my yard digging holes, and poor Peaches was cowering on the porch."

"How is Peaches now?" Jasmine asked politely, fairly certain that the rodent wannabe was just fine.

"He's in the house, in his bed. Recovering."

No, he wasn't. He was on the back of the sofa, peering out the window behind Mrs. Thorpe, his damp nose making marks on the glass. Jasmine didn't point that out. She wanted to calm Mrs. Thorpe down, not get her dander up.

"I'll send Tony here when he gets home. He'll take care of the damage." She got a bit of perverse satisfaction out of not telling her that Tony was her renter. She found it interesting that Mrs. Thorpe would believe that someone like her would be living with a man like Tony DeMonte. She had a feeling that the kind of women Tony hung out with likely wore spandex and perhaps a sequin or two. Jasmine owned neither. And she didn't socialize with men like Tony.

"You do that. I'll be calculating a bill for the damages."

"I'll tell him."

"As soon as he gets home."

"I promise. And, Mrs. Thorpe? If he doesn't pay for the damages, I will."

JASMINE WAS DRESSING for her date with Sean when Tony pulled up to the curb and got out of his car. She went out on the porch to waylay him.

"We need to talk," she said as he approached.

"What about?"

"Your dog."

"How bad?"

"Bad enough. Mrs. Thorpe."

"Mrs…?"

"The lady next door. Muttzilla jumped the fence today and terrorized her dog."

"I'll bet it was the other way around."

"Well, you'll have to convince Mrs. Thorpe of that. And you have a few holes to fill. She's waiting for your call."

"Great."

"I don't want to be at odds with the neighbors. She's really a pretty nice lady."

"I'll make it better."

"I'm sure you will. And wear pants." She noticed then that Tony was studying her. "What?"

"Nothing. You look good."

"Oh. Thank you," Jasmine muttered stiffly, a little uncomfortable that he was noticing her appearance. She pushed her bracelet a little farther up her arm. "I have to go."

"Big date?" Tony asked, his gaze traveling over her black lace sheath, which was the finest article of clothing she owned, then lingering for a moment on the thick gold band on her arm. She squelched the urge to ask him if the bracelet was too much. He probably wouldn't know.

"Yes."

"With that J.Crew guy?"

"It's not really any of your business."

He leaned a shoulder against the gatepost, way too comfortable with himself, and for some reason that made her all the more aware of him, which annoyed her.

"No. It's not," he agreed. "Guess it's just the cop in me wanting answers."

Jasmine didn't like the feeling that he was secretly laughing at her for going out with Sean. "Well, the cop in you can go…jump in the lake."

He laughed for real and Jasmine bristled. "Why don't you go talk to Mrs. Thorpe." She opened her front door and stepped inside, making an effort not to slam the door.

As she passed the window, she had the satisfaction of seeing Mrs. Thorpe leaving her house.

Hopefully, that lady would wipe the smile off Officer DeMonte's face.

A BEER WOULD HAVE been good, but all he had time for was a couple of swigs of Gatorade before going out to intercept the poodle lady. He knew she was approaching—he'd seen her let herself out of her gate as he had rounded the corner to the basement entrance.

He tried to look like an upstanding citizen when he strolled back around the house, but from the expression she wore as she marched toward him he figured it probably wasn't working. He was also glad Muttzilla was safely locked in his room—this woman might be angry enough to call the pound on him. Fortunately, he had an in with animal control, but he'd have a lot less hassle if he could just talk his way out of this.

"Are you that big dog's owner?" Mrs. Thorpe said after stopping next to Jasmine's kitchen window. Tony hoped Jasmine wasn't watching.

"Yes, ma'am."

"Is he licensed?"

"Not in this town, but he is licensed." Tony rested his hands lightly on his hips as he waited for more interrogation, which he sensed was coming.

"Why not this town?"

"We're temporary."

"What does that mean?"

"I'll be moving home in a few weeks."

"Are you a student?" she queried in a skeptical tone. He pulled out his badge, which he'd jammed into his pocket just in case. The woman blinked at it. "You're a police officer?"

"Yes."

Her eyes narrowed with satisfaction. "Then you have a decent paycheck and should be able to afford restitution."

"I should, but I don't," he said truthfully.

"Why not?"

"You want to know my personal business?"

She wore an I-wouldn't-mind expression, so he told her the truth, plain and simple.

"Because I pay my mother's mortgage. She was scammed on an investment scheme and lost a good chunk of her pension. I'm helping her out."

Mrs. Thorpe considered that for a moment. Tony thought she was close to letting herself be swayed, since his story involved a mother being scammed, and he was prepared to elaborate.

"Good story, but it won't work."

"No?" He was surprised at the steel in her voice. This little old lady had backbone.

"No. I want reimbursement and you're not going to sweet-talk me out of it."

"I'll fix your yard."

"I want money to hire someone I trust to fix the yard."

"Let me do it. If you don't like it, you can hire someone."

"I want it fixed by Sunday afternoon and I want the holes resodded, not seeded."

"You got it."

TONY HAD ANOTHER TRIP to the garden store. Pretty soon he'd be on the owner's Christmas-card list.

He was in his room, comparing the strands of grass he'd collected from Mrs. Thorpe's yard with the photos in the horticulture book he'd picked up at the library the previous day, when he heard the clatter of heels on the basement stairs.

Jasmine with a load of laundry. Before her big date, no less. Go figure. The woman was hell on wheels with laundry. He was sometimes tempted to put his own laundry in a pile outside his door just to see what happened. Of course, he'd also probably have to schedule it in that planner she kept so meticulously. She would have made an excellent investigator.

He heard her open and shut the washing machine lid, turn dials, and then a few seconds later the old machine started gushing water into the tub.

Tony knew from experience that in about three minutes the agitator would begin its noisy job, and not long after that, he'd be experiencing the spin cycle, which vibrated his walls as it almost put the ancient machine into orbit.

But today the spin cycle didn't kick in. Instead, he heard Jasmine come back downstairs, open the lid, spin dials and then say a word he'd never heard her utter before. She didn't exactly curse from the gut, but she showed a passing familiarity with the word. Apparently, even upstanding citizens had their moments.

He made himself stay in his room. If she needed help, she would call.

"Tony!"

She needed help. He stuck his head out the door.

"Problem?"

Her eyes were wide and a little wild. "The water won't drain."

Tony stepped past her to peer inside the tub. Definitely full of water.

"I have to have some of the stuff in there tomorrow," Jasmine said. She pressed her lips together as she studied the machine and Tony had a feeling she was on the verge of saying that word again.

"I'll take care of it."

"Are you certain?" she asked in that disbelieving tone of hers, the one that got his back up. He might not have a lot of home-repair experience, having never owned a home, but he wasn't a moron. He knew how to dial Yates's number.

"I'm sure. Go on your date. Just…" She cocked her head, waiting for him to finish the sentence. "Don't do anything I wouldn't do."

Her eyebrows arched. "That gives me carte blanche, doesn't it?"

"Pretty much."

She trotted back up the steps, her heels once again clicking on the wood. She hesitated at the top as though having second thoughts, then the door shut and Tony dug in his pocket for his phone.

"Yeah, I'll help," Yates said with a heavy dose of irony after Tony had outlined the predicament. "Are we on for bowling?"

"We're on," Tony said. He was going bowling with the cousin. *Georgia.* The things he did to preserve his living arrangement.

"Sounds like the pump is clogged," Yates said after Tony described the symptoms. The front door opened and closed above him. Jasmine was off on her date with Sean. Good old Sean. Something about that guy bothered him. Maybe it was the practiced handshake—or maybe he just hated to think about those hands roaming over Jasmine.

"What do I do?"

"First, can you tell me what kind of agitator you have…"

It didn't take long for Tony, following Yates's instructions to get to the root of the matter. Something small and white was jammed into the pump mechanism.

Tony patiently dug it free, using the screwdriver from Jasmine's tool set, then slowly pulled the cloth back into shape. A tiny triangle shape.

"Find the problem?"

"Yeah. I think I'm good."

And more than a little amazed. Who would have thought that Jasmine wore underwear like this?

The lacy bit of cloth barely qualified as undies.

"Thanks. I owe you," Tony said, still regarding the tiny thong dangling from his index finger as he disconnected the phone.

Clearly those grandma panties on the clothesline were decoys. He wondered where she kept the good stuff.

And when she wore it.

He knew then that he would never look at his landlady in the same way again.

CHAPTER EIGHT

"SO WHAT DO YOU THINK?" Sean asked as he and Jasmine stood before the ceiling-high abstract painting.

His company reception was being held in one of her favorite galleries, and many of the paintings would be auctioned off for charity later that evening.

"Gorgeous."

"Yes." His voice was low and intimate.

They moved on to the next work, their shoulders lightly touching as they stood before it. Jasmine lifted a glass of wine to her lips and sipped.

"I like this one even better," she said. The painting was not as large as the previous one, but more striking, with a bold swirl of purple seeping into feathery strokes of blue and white, complemented by seemingly random touches of yellow. The work reminded Jasmine of her black eye, now almost completely healed, but she kept that to herself.

"I plan to bid on it."

"Really?"

"Mmm-hmm." Sean kept his gaze on the painting. "I want to start collecting."

"This would be a good starting point," Jasmine said. "I like it." And she had a feeling it would go for a healthy sum.

Sean introduced Jasmine to his boss just before dinner.

"So you're Richard Storm's daughter."

"Yes, I am," she said, well versed in her role. She offered her hand, smiled warmly. Sean seemed to swell a little beside her.

"And a librarian by trade."

"Yes. To my father's great disappointment, business and economics did not interest me."

"So you put your future in books."

She smiled again and quoted, "'The greatest university of all is a collection of books.'"

The man nodded. "Thomas Carlyle. I have quite a library of my own, you know."

"Really?" Jasmine said. "First editions?"

"Several…"

JASMINE WAS SMILING as she let herself into the house several hours later. Ghengis emerged from her bedroom, stretching as he walked. He was recovering from his injury and was in a pleasant mood for once. He bumped his head affectionately against her leg.

"Yes, I had a good time," Jasmine said. "Thanks for asking."

Sean's boss had sat with them during dinner, discussing literature and various first editions he owned or coveted, and Jasmine had enjoyed the way the dinner conversation revolved around a subject in which she was well informed, as opposed to business microcosms or the latest economic theories. The only rough spot had been when Sean had not won the bid for the purple painting and had gone silent, but he recovered when the dancing started, and the evening had ended as well as it had begun.

Jasmine changed out of her dress; then, humming to herself, headed down the basement steps, wondering if Tony had had any luck with the washing machine. She snapped on the light at the bottom of the stairs, and her eyes rounded as she saw her smallest thong—her missing thong—attached to the clothesline by a single wooden pin.

It didn't take a brain surgeon to figure out what had been clogging the drain mechanism.

Jasmine groaned as she snatched the wisp of underwear off the line and headed back for the stairs. She'd be washing her delicates by hand from now on.

Tony's door opened before she'd made three steps. She kept climbing, but Tony said her name and she stopped. "Would it be all right if Mutt spent the night outside?" Tony asked. "I know it's not his turn—"

"I'll keep Ghengis inside," she said, hoping to escape. No such luck.

"Thanks." Tony stepped into view at the bottom of the stairs, his gaze zeroing in on the thong clutched in her hand. Jasmine chose to face the situation with equanimity.

"I see you found the problem with the washer," she said, tilting her chin up slightly.

"Yeah, I did."

"I'm impressed."

His mouth curved. "So am I." There was no mistaking his meaning.

"Then I guess we're even," Jasmine said coolly. "Good night, Officer DeMonte."

There was humor in his tone as he said, "Good night, Miss Storm."

ELISE HAD FINALLY MADE some headway with Andy, having taken the initiative and asked him out to a movie. He'd accepted, and now she was nervously awaiting the night.

"I enjoy talking to him," she said as she and Jasmine collected the books from the exterior book drop the morning of the big date, "but date talk is different than work talk, you know?"

"I know." Jasmine gave Elise an armload of books, which she then loaded onto the cart they used for transport. "Let him talk about himself. Guys like that."

"Not Andy," Elise said, pushing her glasses up.

"So what do you talk about?"

"Work. Books. History. What Chad's done lately that's weird." Elise closed the lid of the book drop. "I don't think that Andy has much family. When I talk about mine, he doesn't answer back. The only thing I know is that his father was a teacher."

"I know someone else who responds in much the same way."

"Sean?"

"No." She was aware of Sean's life story—professor father, lawyer mother, only child. "Tony."

"The cop in the basement?"

"The same."

"Why do you want information about his family?"

"I don't." Which she realized, to her surprise, wasn't exactly true. She was curious about him. "I just mean that he talks, but he doesn't give much information about himself unless I *ask*. Try asking."

"All right."

"So are you guys meeting after work?" Jasmine said,

bringing the subject back to the momentous first date. Andy was not working that afternoon, although he usually did work Fridays, and Jasmine sincerely hoped he wouldn't stand her friend up.

"Yes. At seven. At the theater. Then we'll take it from there."

"I guess after tonight you'll find out if this egg is going to hatch."

"Yes," Elise said excitedly. "I guess so." She seemed a lot more confident than she'd been a few days ago.

SEAN CALLED SHORTLY AFTER she got off work, apologized for short notice and then asked if she would mind going out to dinner with his boss and a few associates later that evening. Jasmine had no problem with dinner in a nice restaurant with a man who enjoyed talking about books.

But the evening turned out somewhat differently from the previous one. This one was more business than pleasure, and Jasmine soon understood that she was there more so that Sean wouldn't be the odd person at the table than as a member of the group. The discussion centered around an upcoming business conference that coincided with her father's awards banquet.

Sean brought her dad's name up several times and Jasmine began to wonder if what Sean really wanted was a connection, and then told herself she was being petty. She was just touchy about this stuff because it had interfered with her life so much while she'd been growing up.

"So do you have any big plans when your father visits?" his boss asked as they waited for their coffee.

Jasmine thought she'd be lucky if she saw him for more

than the banquet and one duty luncheon. "I'm still not certain what his schedule is," she replied diplomatically.

"But he's staying with you, isn't he?" the boss's wife asked.

"Probably not. He's allergic to dogs." That sounded better than he prefers a hotel.

"Oh, what kind of dog do you have?"

"I think he's a Great Dane."

"You think?" the boss asked on a laugh. "How could you not know?"

"He actually belongs to…a friend." Jasmine smiled tightly as she felt Sean go tense beside her. "I'm just keeping him for a short time until he—my friend, that is—finds a place to live. I have a big fenced yard."

"How nice," the boss's wife said, dabbing at her lips before placing the napkin beside her plate.

The topic shifted then, much to Jasmine's relief, but it was not dead. Sean resurrected it on the way home.

"*Are* you becoming friends with the man in your basement?" he inquired with studied casualness as he turned down her street.

Jasmine glanced over, surprised. "I hardly know him," she said truthfully. "But if I did decide to be friends with him, do you have a problem with that?"

"No," Sean said lightly, but Jasmine didn't really believe him. "Although it is kind of hard to have a woman you're interested in living with another guy."

"I'm not living with him," Jasmine said in a clipped tone.

"I realize you're not *living* with him, but he is very…*close*."

Jasmine shifted her gaze to stare straight ahead out

the windshield as he pulled the car to the curb in front of her house, debating how to handle the situation.

He had a point—she was living in close contact with another man. And, in a way, it was flattering that Sean was concerned. But in another way…in another way, she didn't feel comfortable with his concern.

He lightly touched her shoulder, and she turned to look at him. He didn't speak and after a few seconds of silent contemplation, she said, "You have nothing to worry about. You couldn't ask for two people more different than he and I."

"Not a case of opposites attracting, then?"

"More a case of me not liking jealousy."

Sean's expression clouded and then he said, "I'll work on it."

"I'd like that."

JASMINE FELT RESTLESS the next morning, her day off, and it was because of Sean. She hated to admit that the guy who had appeared so perfect in the beginning suddenly was a little less so.

And what bothered her most was that she couldn't put her finger on exactly what bothered her. Something was off. Maybe the twinge of jealousy he'd shown regarding Tony. Or maybe the fact that he'd dropped her father's name about a dozen times the night before.

Or maybe it was all her imagination. Even if it wasn't, he was human, for heaven's sake, and allowed to have faults, like everyone else. He had more than enough good points to compensate for a few less-than-perfect ones.

She went into the kitchen and got the remainder of a loaf of French bread, and stuffed it into a paper bag before exiting the house and walking the three blocks to the park. There she spent a good fifteen minutes sitting on the bench next to the pond, slowly tearing the loaf apart and tossing bits of it to the ducks and seagulls.

The bread was gone except for the last tough bit of the heel, when the birds suddenly scattered, squawking and protesting, as a giant dog galloped through them, then slid to a stop.

"Mutt?" The dog was dragging a leash and panting around the ball he held in his teeth. The man who jogged up from behind was breathing hard, too.

"'Morning." The damp air had separated Tony's hair into individual curls, and he resembled a Roman soldier in sweat pants. "He kind of got away from me."

"You run?"

"Almost every day."

"I had no idea you woke that early."

He made a wry face at her.

Mutt dropped the ball on her white athletic shoe, leaving a muddy mark. Jasmine wrinkled her nose.

"It went in the pond," Tony explained.

"So it's not dog slobber?"

"Not all of it."

Jasmine reached down to pick up the damp ball, then threw it across the field, wiping her hand on her pants as soon as she released it. Tony followed the trajectory, clearly impressed.

"I played softball in high school."

"You haven't lost your arm."

"Not through lack of trying. I haven't played in a long time."

"You don't look like the softball type."

"Oh, really? What type do I look like?"

"Bookworm."

"Be careful of stereotypes," she said automatically as Muttzilla came back and dropped the ball at her feet, looking hopefully at her and then at the ball. The scratch on his nose was beginning to heal.

"What's stereotypical?" Tony started down the path and Jasmine fell in step. Muttzilla took the ball in his mouth and followed. "It's logical," he continued. "Librarian...bookworm..."

"Cop...doughnut."

He patted his flat abdomen. "No doughnuts here."

She had to admit he had a point. She'd seen him without his shirt and the guy was as lean as a rail. But not scrawny lean—taut-muscle lean. Must be all that running he said he was doing.

"I *am* a bookworm," she admitted. "A bookworm who likes to play softball."

"And I'm a cop who dislikes doughnuts."

"I had you pegged as a bona fide junk-food junkie."

"Takeout doesn't always mean junk."

"I've seen the boxes in the trash," she said dryly. *"Ed's House of Chicken?"*

"It's not doughnuts."

"And it's not healthy."

"I can cook, actually. Entire meals, if need be. Healthy ones."

"When's the last time you cooked a healthy meal?" she asked on a challenging note.

"It's been a while, but I cooked a lot when I was growing up."

"Really?"

"If I hadn't, we wouldn't have had meals on the days my mom was on shift. She taught me the rudiments of cooking, then bought the groceries and turned me loose. The rest I did on my own."

"Where'd you grow up?"

"Seattle."

Mutt pushed his way in between them, looking up at Jasmine. She scratched his head but didn't go for the ball, so after a few seconds he ran on ahead.

"How long have you had Muttzilla?"

"Hmm…about six months now."

"Is that all? He seems devoted to you."

"He is."

"Ah, the humble owner."

"We kind of saved each other's lives."

Jasmine frowned over at him, curious. "How?"

"He belonged to a drug dealer, and I was one of the dealer's regulars."

"Really?" She tried not to sound shocked.

"*Pretend* really," Tony answered patiently. "I'd been on that job for almost a year, and I got to know the dog. In fact, I treated him better than his owner did. The guy tended to kick him a lot. And then… when the final deal went down, the one where the arrests would be made, things fell apart. Somehow I got made."

"Found out?"

"Found out."

"What happened?"

"Fortunately, it happened shortly before the cavalry arrived. The dealer decided he was going to shoot me and the dog decided he wasn't. Muttzilla jumped the guy."

Jasmine put a hand to her mouth. "You're kidding, right?"

"Actually, the dealer kicked Mutt to get him out of the way and that was when the Mutt jumped him, but it still saved me. See that nasty scar on Mutt's back leg?"

She nodded mutely.

"Bullet wound."

They walked for a few minutes in silence as Jasmine digested what he had just told her. "Do you have any…aftereffects? I mean from almost being shot?"

"They're pretty much gone now. I was lucky. This stuff bothers some guys more than others. My partner…he didn't come out of it so well."

"Why? Did he almost get shot, too?"

"No. His problem was that he quit pretending to use."

"Oh." Jasmine plucked a tall piece of grass from the edge of the trail and bent it between her fingers. "How's he doing now?"

"He's working on recovery. Long process."

"What about you saving the dog's life? How did that happen?"

"The powers-that-be wanted to have him put down, but I smuggled him away before they could do it."

Jasmine smiled. She could imagine Tony doing that, and now she understood why he sacrificed for his dog.

Tony smiled back—the same carefree smile she'd seen the day he moved in—and it made her heart bump. *That* wasn't in the plan. Nor was the fact that, even after running, he smelled good to her. Musky and masculine, in a way that made her senses hum with awareness.

She was *not* going to continue to foster this…*what-ever* it was. Tony DeMonte lived exactly the kind of life she was trying to avoid—one fraught with uncertainty. And he appeared to thrive on it.

"Something wrong?" Tony asked.

She glanced up at him, hoping she didn't look guilty. "Just wondering…have you ever done anything other than law enforcement?" she asked.

"Nope."

"Have you told many people this story?"

"Nope. My motto is only tell what you need to, then you don't get into trouble."

"I'm not trouble."

"We'll see."

TONY HAD THE FEELING from her startled expression that Jasmine had never been referred to as *trouble*. He was fairly certain she was the opposite of trouble and well aware of it—the kind of person who studied for driver's tests, calculated taxes on January fourteenth instead of April fourteenth. Which was pretty much the antithesis of the way he lived, hanging on by his toes.

"What's so funny?" she asked with a touch of defensiveness.

He looked down, noticing that she had a faint sprinkle of freckles across the bridge of her nose, and that they looked rather charming on someone so serious. "Nothing."

"I bet."

They left the path bordering the pond—the same one Tony had tackled the suspect in—and started across the common. Years had passed—like about twenty—since he'd walked in a park with a woman, and he liked it. The sun, the grass, the dog bounding around them, hopeful that Jasmine would throw the ball again. It was time to ruin the moment.

"I need a favor." He watched her as he spoke, reading her reaction. She appeared surprised, but other than that, so far, so good.

"What's that?"

"Would you go bowling with me?"

Her mouth fell open. "Bowling?"

"Don't look so horrified," he said, making a mental note to never ask her out for real. The idea obviously did not appeal.

"I'm not horrified. I'm confused. Why do you need me to go bowling with you?"

"Protection. My partner's wife is attempting to set me up. If I show up with a date, then maybe she'll give up."

"Maybe you should show up with your dog."

He laughed. "That might work, but what if she's an animal lover?"

"I can't do this to some lonely woman."

"I've met this woman, and trust me, she's not lonely. Her ego keeps her company." He'd gotten a glimpse of Melanie's cousin when he stopped by Yates's place to borrow a hedge trimmer. She appeared to have a forceful personality; in fact, he was close to believing that she could take him in a fair fight. Not someone he wanted to tangle with unless he was seriously interested. And he wasn't.

"I don't think so."

"Trust me, this setup will not work for either me or the woman involved. You'd be saving everyone a lot of pain." *Especially him.*

"Tony…"

"You *can* bowl, can't you?"

She nodded slowly. "I—"

"Read a book on it," he guessed.

"I attended a class."

"Almost as bad," Tony said. He had a feeling that he'd be bowling with Georgia on Saturday night. He just hoped he wouldn't be defending his virtue later in the evening.

"What's wrong with attending a class?" Jasmine asked after a few seconds of silence.

"Sometimes you have to just wade in and *do* things. You know, experience them extemporaneously."

"Pretty big word for a cop."

"We know some really big words. Methamphetamine. *Cannabis sativa.*"

"Cinnamon apple turnover."

"We've been over that."

The words were barely out of his mouth when Jasmine froze, her gaze fixed on a dark-haired man in glasses, who was getting out of a red sports car in the parking lot.

"What?" Tony asked, settling a hand on her shoulder. Her body was tense.

"Just a guy I don't like being around."

"What's his name?"

"Brenton Elwood."

He seemed harmless enough, which meant absolutely jack. Some of the most violent men he'd ever known looked harmless.

"How do you know him?"

"The library. I help him with research on his family

tree. He's asked me out a few times, but I told him I didn't feel comfortable dating patrons."

"Do you think he might be the guy in your garage?"

"The thought has crossed my mind."

Brenton settled on the grass next to the pond, and Tony slipped his arm around Jasmine's shoulders, turning her in the opposite direction.

"I'll check him out. Let's go home."

"All right."

They walked a few steps in tandem until Jasmine moved away, but she did it nicely, casually, not as though she hated being touched by him. And because she was the one who'd moved away, his gut instinct was to follow, to pursue.

He squelched the impulse. Thong or no thong, she was not his type. But she wasn't quite what he'd predicted she was, either. Jasmine could play—when she let herself. But for some reason she didn't.

"Tell what you don't like about him."

"It's just a...feeling."

"I believe in trusting feelings."

"Unless they involve people being in your house?" she asked with exaggerated innocence.

"Look—"

She held up a hand, cutting him off. "I know that logically there's no proof. I also know what I'm feeling. It may be my imagination, but I'm going with it. Okay?" She focused on the ground and said stubbornly, "Even if does make me look like a crazy cat lady."

"Maybe you *are* a crazy cat lady," he said and was glad she was fighting a smile instead of taking offense. He settled his hand on the back of her neck for a moment, then reached out to snag Mutt's leash as he trotted by.

"I'll go bowling with you," Jasmine said quietly as they approached the street.

"Excuse me?" He really hoped he wasn't hearing things.

She stopped walking and faced him, her expression sincere and direct and…gorgeous. "I'll go bowling with you."

"Why?" *That's it, Tony. Give her an opportunity to reconsider. Cut your own throat.*

"Because it won't kill me to go bowling with you and you need a favor. Any more questions?"

"Not one."

"Then let's go home."

And as he walked home with Jasmine, for the first time in a long time Tony wished he were someone other than who he was…that he were someone who could walk in the park with a nice lady without knowing that nothing could ever come of it—just because of who he was and what he did for a living.

CHAPTER NINE

NEITHER ELISE NOR ANDY was at work the next day, so Jasmine did not get to hear about the big date; however, Brenton *was* there.

Jasmine forced herself to approach him and ask if he needed help with research, watching his reaction as she did so. He seemed his usual arrogant, oblivious self, certain that Jasmine found him attractive, certain that he was doing her a favor by letting her help him, which she did for almost half an hour. And while she was helping him, she tried to key into her subconscious and see if anything about him triggered a bit of memory—a mannerism of his, or a scent, or…anything.

Nothing.

She didn't think he was the one, but regardless, she was going to err on the side of caution and he was going to continue to be a suspect.

She didn't hear a word from Sean all day. Somehow she wasn't surprised, which made it all that much easier to go home and slide into a pair of jeans and a sweater in preparation for her bowling date with Tony. No. Not a date. She was doing him a favor.

Bowling with a narcotics agent. Weird how life worked out sometimes.

And it was interesting how often she thought about walking in the park with his arm around her—like…well, a couple. And what a strange couple they made—although, she had to admit, she couldn't remember a time when she'd felt so… She closed her eyes, searched her vocabulary. *Secure.* Yes, that was the word she was looking for. Secure.

JASMINE MIGHT NOT HAVE been a regular in the bowling alley, but she was game. She'd winced at the noise level when they'd first entered the building, but by the time she'd put on the spiffy multicolored rented shoes a bored kid had handed to her over the counter, she seemed to have acclimated.

She took her time choosing the perfect ball, testing several, then marched up to the lane when Tony told her they'd bowl a practice game while they waited for Yates and Melanie, since he was rusty. After studying the pins for a few seconds, Jasmine adopted a careful stance, then began her approach. She let the ball go at exactly the wrong moment, and it sailed into the gutter.

Tony laughed—mainly because he knew he'd probably be doing the same. She straightened her shoulders and did not look at him, though he saw her cast a glance at the people in the neighboring lanes.

"It's been a while," she said darkly. She waited for her ball to return and repeated the performance—only this time the ball swung out close to the gutter, then arced neatly back to sail directly toward the pins. A perfect hook. A perfect strike.

He let out a low whistle. "I think maybe I should have taken bowling class."

"What's your technique?"

"I aim for the center pin."

"Well, if you hook the ball—"

"I aim for the center pin."

"Hey, Tony!" Tony swung around to see Yates hailing him as he moved through the crowd of kids surrounding the concession stand. "Starting without us?"

"We thought we'd have a practice game."

"We?" Melanie asked. She was a petite woman, with dark hair and dimpled cheeks.

"Yeah, we?" Yates echoed grimly, holding his rented shoes in one hand.

"I brought someone," Tony said innocently. "I thought I was supposed to."

"You must have misunderstood," Yates said through his teeth as his wife sent him a look. "Nice to see you again, Jasmine."

"I didn't think you'd remember my name," Jasmine said with a smile.

"You're the first librarian I ever tried to bust, so, yeah, I remembered your name."

Melanie was obviously growing less and less happy with each passing moment, so Yates briefly explained how he and Tony and Jasmine had met.

"And now you're dating?" Melanie asked Tony.

"I'm living with her," Tony said, hoping Jasmine wouldn't correct the assumption. She poked her thumb into the back of his thigh, but kept her mouth shut when she excused herself to finish her frame. He owed her.

"I guess I didn't understand the situation." Melanie reached into her bag for her cell phone. "If you will excuse me for a second."

"I'm going to get skinned alive, but you're safe," Yates said morosely as his wife walked over by the shoe counter to speak into the phone.

"Better you than me," Tony agreed, settling into a molded plastic chair. A kid darted by on his way to the next lane, barely missing Yates, who then slapped his bowling shoes onto the small table next to where Tony sat.

"I'll have to devise a plan to make your life miserable," he muttered as he bent to untie his street shoes.

"I wouldn't even notice more misery," Tony replied, watching Jasmine rack up a spare. He didn't want to disappoint her as her teammate but had a strong feeling he was going to.

"Georgia is coming down anyway," Melanie told Yates when she returned.

"Georgia?" Tony asked innocently, ignoring Yates.

"My cousin. She's a paramedic on the ambulance squad. I thought you'd met her."

"The redhead?" Tony asked. "We didn't actually meet. I just said hello as I was leaving. Paramedic, you say?" Jasmine walked over to stand next to his chair.

"Your turn," she said.

Tony took a chance and casually hooked a finger in her center back belt loop, trying to maintain the couple facade so that Melanie would give up once and for all. Thankfully, Jasmine didn't smack him.

Instead, she settled a hand on his shoulder, leaned down close to his ear and whispered in a sweet tone, "If your hand goes any lower, you'll be a sorry man."

He softly grunted in acknowledgment. Melanie frowned over at them, and then Tony let go of Jasmine's belt and went to take his turn in the lanes.

JASMINE RECOGNIZED GEORGIA from around town. She was a distinctive woman—tall, curvaceous, redheaded. She was also opinionated. And usually right—or thought she was. Jasmine had been corrected several times, as had Melanie. Tony was smart enough to keep his mouth shut. But as the evening progressed, Jasmine found herself warming up to Georgia. She was one of those people who got less abrasive as she became more secure with a situation.

By the time the evening drew to a close, the three women were debating whether high heels were a symbol of control—and if so, who was controlling whom?

"Scintillating conversation," Tony commented later as he escorted Jasmine up her walk.

"That's the most fun I've had in a long time."

"You don't get out much, do you?" he asked as he waited for her to find her key in her purse.

"I get out."

"Yeah? Where? The Librarians Ball?"

"Remember that you're talking to the woman who saved your bacon."

"Yeah. You're right. Sorry."

Jasmine glanced up at him after unlocking her door. "Would you like some tea or something?"

He seemed a touch startled at the suggestion, and then a look of dawning comprehension crossed his features. "You want me to check your closets?"

"Am I that transparent?" Even with Tony in the basement, she felt nervous entering a supposedly empty house after dark. "Never mind. I have to get used to checking my own closets."

"I'll check them." He smiled crookedly after following her inside. "I thought maybe you had designs on me."

"And if I did?" Jasmine asked, rising to the challenge because he didn't expect her to.

"I'm saving myself for Ms. Right."

"Which is not me," Jasmine instantly agreed, dropping her keys into the bowl by the door and wondering why those words stung just a little. "Unless you can squeeze yourself into a business suit and do a nine-to-five stint."

"Is that what you want?" Tony asked. "A nine-to-fiver?"

She had assumed that would have been obvious. "It's what I have to have," she replied truthfully.

"I'm allergic to those hours."

Jasmine smiled. "Then I guess we're doomed."

"Good thing you have The Suit," Tony said, his eyes crinkling at the corners.

"Yes. I'm very lucky. And now I'm going to make tea." She headed for the kitchen, feeling more self-conscious than she'd felt all evening—even when Tony had startled her by grabbing her belt loop in that intimate way. Tony followed her as far as the hallway, where they parted company as he began his mission to check closets.

"All clear," he said when he entered the kitchen a few minutes later.

"Thanks. And I did have fun tonight. Georgia is a riot, but I can't believe Melanie envisioned you two together."

"She'd consider anyone with the proper equipment below the belt suitable," Tony said. "That's the only reason I can think of for Melanie trying to set Georgia up with a cop."

"What's wrong with a cop?" Jasmine put the teakettle under the faucet.

"Well, according to Yates, his wife doesn't love the law enforcement life."

"Something did seem a little…off."

"Yeah. She wants to have a kid, but doesn't like the odds of raising it alone."

"Can't say that I blame her."

"And it's not easy being a cop's kid, either."

"Was your dad was a cop?"

"My mom. I followed in her footsteps."

She glanced up as the water overfilled the kettle. "When you said you'd cooked because your mom was on shift, I assumed you meant in a factory or something." She turned the water off and dumped out the extra.

"Nope. She was a cop."

"What did your dad do?"

"He raised another family far away from me. I believe he was in retail."

"You believe?" Her profile was to him as she lit the burner.

"When I hit thirteen, I became a bad influence on his 'real' kids, so I wasn't invited over after that."

"That's awful."

"That's life."

"Were you really a bad influence? I mean…what did you do?"

"Honestly? I had a bad attitude. I resented what my brothers and sister had, because I didn't have anything close. So I was sullen and uncooperative. But, no, I wasn't urging them to smoke and drink, if that's what you're thinking."

"It was exactly what I was thinking." The truth, though, was so much sadder.

"Don't feel sorry for me. I did fine."

"Wouldn't dream of feeling sorry for you," Jasmine lied. They both jumped at the rap on the front door.

"Are you expecting anyone?"

Jasmine shook her head, so Tony went to the door, opened it and stepped back.

"Sean." Instinctively, Jasmine stepped forward, then stopped when she saw the expression on his face.

He was not smiling. "I should have called."

"I was just going downstairs," Tony said in a brisk tone, picking up the sweatshirt he had tossed onto the sofa.

"No. Don't let me interrupt," Sean said smoothly. He turned without another word and walked out of the house.

A patently uncomfortable silence ensued, and it was obvious that Tony had an opinion about what had just happened. Jasmine hoped it was equally obvious that she did not want to hear it.

"Are you okay?" he finally asked, pushing the front door shut.

"I'm fine. A little embarrassed…" She managed a tiny ego-saving smirk. "Don't worry about it. Do you still want tea?"

"I, uh, think I'll pass."

"Thanks," Jasmine said, because she knew she would have difficulty choking down a cup of tea now that her stomach was in a knot. "I had fun tonight."

Tony tightened his mouth as if he had something to say, but felt it would not be well received. Finally he said a quiet good-night as he opened the basement door.

After Tony had descended the steps, Jasmine returned to the stove and snapped off the burner, wondering how a pleasant night could have ended so badly—and how the rest of the situation would play out.

Should she call Sean in the morning and protest her innocence?

Not on her life.

If she and Sean were to have any kind of a future relationship, he would have to trust her. If he didn't—well, much as she hated to admit it, that was that.

ON SUNDAY, TONY COVERED a shift for another guy who had a family. Weekends had never meant much to Tony as far as doing the family thing. His mom had done shifts, so days off were when they happened, and her idea of a family activity had been to tell Tony when to have dinner ready.

Melanie had halfway forgiven Yates, since Georgia had managed to catch the eye of some cop named Bill at the bowling alley, who'd stopped by to shoot the breeze and had been tanked up enough to find Georgia's aggressive attitude as a challenge rather than a turnoff. And— saints be praised—the guy had asked her out again.

Tony was officially off the hook, Yates was almost out of the doghouse and all was right with the world— except for the part where he'd screwed the pooch with Jasmine's beau.

He felt bad about that. Jasmine seemed to like the guy, though he had no idea why. The Nordic god might fit nicely into her lifestyle, but he was a little too smooth and polished for Tony's tastes.

And…well, there was also the possibility that Tony was just a little jealous.

Guys like Sean got women like Jasmine. The Tonys

of the world didn't—because of lifestyle reasons if
nothing else. On top of that, relationships didn't run in
his family. Not on the maternal side, anyway, and that
was the side he took after. Neither career nor disposi-
tion lent itself to happily ever after and he wasn't going
to ruin Jasmine's life. Not after watching a nice guy like
Yates make his wife unhappy. Or, worst-case scenario,
seeing what Gabe's life choices were doing to a tough
girl like Val.

Nope. He wouldn't do that, no matter how strongly
he felt. He liked Jasmine too much.

Because there'd been an increase in after-hours store
robberies, Tony spent most of his shift cruising down
the alleys. He was reiterating to himself the reasons
Jasmine was off-limits, when he noticed one of Jasmine's acquaintances—the man he'd just checked out
and found to be clean on paper.

Brenton Elwood was strolling toward the rear of a
shop that specialized in upscale sex toys—blown glass
in artsy forms—as well as other intimate accoutrements.
The guy went in the alley entrance. Nothing illegal
about that. Tony pulled in behind a Dumpster and
waited.

Five minutes later Elwood emerged with a tasteful
black paper bag and went back the way he'd come.

No laws broken, but Tony filed the info away for
future use.

The shift was as quiet as any he'd had in Mondell—
possibly because it was Sunday. And rainy. No one felt
like robbing a store in the daylight in the rain. All the
deviants were invisible for the time being. They'd creep
out again at night, when Mondell changed.

When he finally got home after his mind-numbingly boring shift, a nice Audi pulled up to the curb just after he did, and Sean got out.

Okay. Time to make peace, set the record straight. Tony strolled over. The rain had stopped for the moment.

"Hey," Tony said. "The other night…it wasn't what you seemed to think."

The guy looked down his nose at him—or he would have, if Tony hadn't been just a hair taller. The effect was the same, though—it made Tony want to smack him one.

"It really isn't your business."

"I was there, so that kind of makes it my business."

"No," Sean said shortly. "It doesn't." Then he shouldered past Tony and headed for Jasmine's front door.

Tony had been planning to walk the Mutt in the park before it started raining again, but now he thought he'd hang around the place. Just in case Jasmine needed a hand. He'd lend it gladly, especially if she needed it to connect with Sean's jaw.

JASMINE WAS IN THE middle of about a mile of crochet thread that she was unraveling, having found a mistake way back at the beginning that she couldn't live with. Her hair was in an untidy Sunday-afternoon ponytail and she was wearing a T-shirt and old sweats that said Mondell U. across the butt. Just exactly the way she wanted to greet an unexpected visitor. To Sean's credit, he did not give one indication that she was anything but perfect. He seemed to have a talent for that.

"I'm sorry about last night."

"Things happen," she said, holding the door so he couldn't enter the house.

"Can I come in? Please?"

Jasmine debated and then stepped back.

"There was nothing going on with Tony and me," she said as he sat on the opposite end of the sofa. "I told you that before. Either you trust me or you don't."

She continued winding thread into a ball, needing something to focus on other than the man sitting two feet away from her.

"I know that. Now. But the last thing I expected late in the evening was to find...*him*...*here*."

"And you gave me so much time to explain." She took a couple of aggressive wraps around the ball.

"Jasmine. Look at me." She looked. "It was one of those moments where I didn't know how to respond, and so it was best to get out before I did or said something I regretted." His gaze remained intense after he stopped speaking. "Hasn't that ever happened to you?"

"I've been in those situations," Jasmine said.

"I overreacted." His mouth compressed. "I'm very attracted to you, as I'm sure you know. You're classy and intelligent. My boss loves you, and he's no pushover."

"That's good news," she said, happy to hear that she was a business asset. Her father would be *so* proud.

Sean cleared his throat, perhaps realizing that he'd made a faux pas by mentioning his boss. "I'm sorry. This isn't about my boss, and there's really not much else to say, except that I was jealous and shouldn't have been. I freely admit I don't like having the cop in the basement, but it's none of my business. I do trust you."

Jasmine set the ball of thread beside her on the

sofa. "Are you interested in me because I'm Richard Storm's daughter?"

Sean was so patently shocked at the question that she felt ashamed for having asked it. But she still wanted an answer.

"No."

She believed him. "I'm sorry I asked, but…" She was not quite certain how to explain.

"You really thought I was dating you because of your father?" Sean leaned back against the sofa cushions. "Has that happened before?"

"No. But I've never dated anyone who knew him before." Or name-dropped as much as Sean had. "I've never dated anyone in the business community, for that matter."

"Wow. That narrows your options."

"Only to the liberal arts."

They watched each other for a moment and then Sean started to fight a smile. A moment later it broke through and Jasmine felt the tension in her body begin to dissipate.

"I guess I should be flattered that you're dating me." He leveled a serious look at her. "You are still dating me, right?"

"Yes."

"We'll work on things, Jasmine. We have something that's good. It's just a matter of getting the kinks out. I'll work on jealousy and you can work on loving my career. Deal?"

"Deal."

But after Sean left, Jasmine could not shake the un-settled feeling she had. He'd seemed so perfect, was so perfect, but he was beginning to leave her cold.

It made no sense. He was charming and fun, and her father would love him because of his career... *Maybe that was it.* The thing that had been bugging her.

Her hands stilled as she stared off across the room. Maybe she'd become so warped by resenting that her father always put business ahead of his personal commitments that she was transferring those feelings to Sean. The businessman.

Which was not fair to Sean, and not fair to her. She slowly wrapped the thread again. Like Sean had said, she had some things to work out, too.

JASMINE DISCOVERED ON HER monthly movie night with Elise that she and her friend were pretty much at opposite ends of the dating spectrum. Whereas Jasmine's dating life had become a source of stress, Elise's had become a cause for celebration. Things with Andy were coming along nicely.

"For a little while, I thought he might be interested in you," Elise confessed.

"Me?" Jasmine's eyes grew round. *Oh, that would be grand...*

"He asked about you a couple of times—whether you were doing all right after the attack. But I've convinced him you're fine." Elise cast Jasmine a quick look. "You are fine, aren't you?"

Jasmine laughed. "I'm fine. And he was probably just being nice—you know, showing concern for one of your friends?"

"Fortunately, I arrived at the same conclusion," Elise said with a satisfied smile, and then she leaned forward. "How are things with Sean?"

"Good." A corner of Jasmine's mouth quirked before she added, "I hope."

Elise's eyebrows rose. "Explanation, please."

So Jasmine explained. Briefly. "I don't know if this is just one of those bumps people go through at the beginning of a relationship while they're figuring everything out, or if it's more."

"Sounds like a bump," Elise said sagely. "I mean, you can get over the fact that your father will love him, can't you?"

Jasmine smiled wryly at Elise's phrasing. "I guess. It's just that he's a little like my father, you know? And that's coloring my thinking."

"I understand, but now that you've figured it out—" Elise snapped her fingers "—you deal with it. As to the other, what does a guy like Sean have to be jealous of?"

"Tony, apparently."

Elise sputtered into her drink. "I don't think so."

"That's what I told him," Jasmine said darkly. And she hoped that he was paying attention. Tony was about as much threat to him as Andy was.

FUNNY, HOW REALITY COULD have such a sobering effect on a person who up until then had been having a pretty good day. Tony had answered his cell while mowing Jasmine's lawn and then spent almost twenty minutes sitting in the sun on Jasmine's front step with the phone glued to his ear, hammering things out with Parker, his superior in Seattle.

He'd be going out on another task-force assignment when he returned to his old job. Parker wanted to know if Tony thought he was up to another long job—especially after how the last one had ended. Tony said yes. What else could he say? Put me behind a desk? Like there were any of those positions available.

When he hung up the phone, and as he sat studying his nemesis—Jasmine's old cranky lawn mower—he was aware of a bone-deep weariness. Back to the scumbags and scrotes. He had a few more weeks in fantasyland, but that didn't make it any easier to face being flat-ass broke, owing more than he could pay and having next-to-no options employment-wise if he wanted to keep his head above water.

Jasmine opened the gate then, a walking-talking reminder of the other problem with fantasyland. He didn't really fit in.

"Is something wrong?" she said. And then she surprised him by plopping down beside him on the wooden steps.

He managed a smile. "No. Just work."

"Oh." She brushed her hair away from her cheek with one hand. "Did old Betsy quit, or are you letting her rest?" she asked, referring to the lawn mower.

"We both needed a rest. Something wrong with you?"

She looked taken aback, but smiled, charming the hell out of him—an experience that was becoming more common every single day.

"No. I was just thinking how the place will lack a certain liveliness when you and Muttzilla vacate."

"Will you be nervous?"

"Maybe for a while, but—" she wrinkled her nose "—the logical part of my brain says I'll be fine."

"Ever get tired of being logical?"

Her expression shifted. "I never have before, but

lately…" She shook her head with weariness that matched his own. "Well, I'll just have to stick with logic. It's gotten me this far."

"Yeah," Tony agreed ironically. "It's best to stick with what you know."

JASMINE DIDN'T HEAR FROM Sean for two days after he'd stopped by to apologize, so when the phone rang, she half expected it to be him. It wasn't. It was her father.

"I checked on Nielsen," her father told her after a few stiff niceties, as if she would be happy to hear that he was screening the men in her life.

"Thanks, Dad." She hoped the sarcasm wasn't evident. "What did you find out?"

"He is on the guest list, as you suspected."

"Good." Although she'd yet to ask Sean to attend with her.

"He's also quite a go-getter, from what I've been hearing."

"He is very serious about what he does," Jasmine said. Well, she'd called this one correctly—her father seemed to like what he'd heard.

"That's what I understand. In fact, his bosses are quite impressed."

It was rare for Jasmine to hear approval in her father's voice and she couldn't help but enjoy the feeling of warmth that followed. He'd eventually reconciled himself to her getting a degree in English literature, but it had taken a while. It had helped that several of his closest business associates had also lost children to the liberal arts. She was certain, though, that he hated to tell people his only child was a librarian. But if she was having a serious relationship with an MBA—that would make up for a lot.

"Do you have a definite ETA next week?" Jasmine asked, changing the subject while she was ahead. "I was thinking we could go out to dinner."

"That's why I called. The original date isn't going to work. I'll probably have to fly in the morning of the reception instead of the day before. I'll give you some exact times as soon as I have them pinned down. I'm juggling a few things right now." As always.

"All right, Dad."

Sean called less than an hour later. Must be a slow day in the business world, Jasmine mused as she recognized the number and, a few seconds later, the voice.

"There's an encore performance of *Les Misérables* at the university theater on Saturday," he said after a quick hello. "I'd really like it if you'd go with me."

"Les Miz?"

"If you're interested—and there is *nothing* business related about it," he said sincerely. "Then I thought maybe a late dinner at La Traviata, since we didn't get to go before."

"That sounds…doable."

Sean laughed then, relief evident in his voice, and Jasmine found herself smiling.

"I'll pick you up at six o'clock?"

"I'll be waiting."

TONY PLUNGED HIS SHOVEL into the earth along the fence, levered up a chunk of sod, laid it aside, then worked the soil in preparation for flower planting. Muttzilla hadn't dug up anything in more than two weeks and

Tony was going to make good on his promise to leave the backyard much better than he'd found it. He finished that spot and moved to another about two feet away. The guy at the store had said the flowers would widen out, and not to be fooled by how small they were now.

Tony removed another chunk of sod, then stabbed the shovel into the dirt, putting his back into it.

He was worried about Yates.

The kid was working on an ulcer because of that scumbag dealer Davenport, who was still baiting him ever since the failed drug bust. As the owner of a skuzzy electronics store, he'd attended a recent chamber of commerce luncheon where Yates gave yet another presentation. To think of Davenport sitting through the tedium just to bug Yates would have been almost comical, if the scrote had not also pointedly asked about Melanie's health after the meeting.

Yates considered it to be a threat, and Tony agreed that although the guy was probably just messing with Yates's head, Yates shouldn't take chances on the matter, even though there wasn't much that could be done about it.

In a way, Tony was glad he'd never had anyone in his life who could have been used as a means of threatening him. He had his mother, of course, but he pitied the fool who took her on. Very few men had mothers who were as good a shot as his was, and she still went to the range regularly.

"Today I'm going to get Davenport," Yates would announce pleasantly at the beginning of each shift. And at the end of the shift, he'd say, "Tomorrow I'm going to get Davenport."

Tony hoped one of these days the prediction came true. There was still activity around the library. People known to be involved in the drug trade came and went from the house they had raided near the library, but Yates had not been able to convince a judge to issue another search warrant.

Well, at least Jasmine knew enough not to hang out in the alley at night anymore, so if he and Yates ever did do another bust, they probably wouldn't nail librarians.

"Those won't grow, you know."

A strident voice broke into his thoughts, and Tony lifted his head to find Mrs. Thorpe peering at him from over the back gate as he patted soil around the base of one of the flowers.

"Why not?"

"Because you're planting them too deep."

"I am?" He didn't realize there was such a thing as too deep.

The woman rolled her eyes. "Yes. You are."

"You want to show me?"

"Is that...*dog* in the yard?"

She looked around before unlatching the gate and letting herself into the yard, Peaches dancing on the lease beside her. "Is your dog put away?" she repeated.

"Yes. But he wouldn't hurt your dog, you know."

"Peaches is frightened of him, and when Peaches is frightened, he has accidents."

"We can't have that," Tony said solemnly.

Mrs. Thorpe shook her head. "Not when I've just had new flooring laid." She gingerly knelt beside him and picked up the plant. "Now, not all flowers are like this, but do you see this crown here? It has to be aboveground...."

JASMINE COULDN'T BELIEVE her eyes. Tony and Mrs. Thorpe were kneeling close to each other, conferring over a potted plant that Mrs. Thorpe held in one hand. He nodded at something she said, then she carefully eased the plant out of the container and placed it in a hole before patting soil around it.

Tony grinned at the lady and Jasmine's heart did a funny little thump. The guy was kind of growing on her. She was able to talk to him in a way she wasn't yet able to talk to Sean—which didn't make a whole lot of sense, but it did have her thinking.

And since she did not want to disturb Tony and Mrs. Thorpe, or join them, she quietly let herself into the house to get ready for her date, thanking her lucky stars that Muttzilla was apparently downstairs so her arrival went unnoticed.

Tony and Mrs. Thorpe.

Go figure.

SEAN PICKED JASMINE up a half hour before the play, spectacular as always in a custom suit, cut from light-weight navy wool, that perfectly emphasized his Scandinavian coloring. He was definitely a head turner and Jasmine hoped she measured up in her simple black dress that had cost about double what it should have.

They were on their way to their seats when a tall redhead, accompanied by a shorter, rather squarish man, hailed Jasmine. It took her a second to realize the couple was Georgia and Bill.

"They gave tickets to all the ambulance crew members!" Georgia announced. "This is my first stage play."

"I'm an old hand at this," Bill said with a grin. "I

was a snowflake in second grade." Georgia elbowed him and he laughed before holding out a hand to Sean. "Bill Fontana."

"Oh, I'm sorry," Jasmine said before finishing the introductions.

"You look a lot different than you did bowling," Bill said to Jasmine with a wink, and then he grinned jovially at Sean, making Jasmine wonder just how much of a prefunction he and Georgia had indulged in.

"Yes, she cleans up nicely," Sean said without a trace of irony. "Well, we need to be getting to our seats. A pleasure to meet you."

"Yeah. Maybe we'll see you around," Georgia called after them, sounding confident that they would be meeting up soon.

Sean escorted Jasmine a few steps toward the entrance to the seating before he said with careful nonchalance, "I didn't know you bowled."

"Tony needed a partner," she said evenly, refusing to lie about the matter. Sean gave her a cool look. Jasmine remained silent. She refused to justify an innocent evening out.

"Do you belong to a league?" Sean finally asked as they approached their aisle.

"No. He just needed a partner for the evening."

"I see. A partner. For the evening." The way he said it sounded nasty and Jasmine's spine stiffened.

"Stop, Sean."

"I can't help it. I'm getting a little tired of this guy being such a big part of your life."

"One night bowling is hardly a *big part of my life*. And I thought you said that you trusted me."

"But I thought you understood that it bothers me when you spend time with him."

"This happened *before* you stormed out of my house that night. He's just a friend."

Sean coughed in a way that irritated Jasmine more than a rebuttal would have.

"Hey, at least I have a good time when I'm with him," she said in a low voice.

"How good of a time?" Sean asked.

"What do you mean?"

"Is he getting laid when I'm not?"

Jasmine froze, not quite believing what he had just said, or how rapidly the situation had snowballed out of control. She would have loved to be the kind of woman who could slap a face and walk away, but she'd never hit anyone in her life and she was not about to start. So instead, she tossed the end of her stole over her shoulder and, just before turning to head for the nearest exit, said the first thing that popped into her mind.

"He has a much better shot at it than you do."

CHAPTER TEN

THE TAXI HOME HAD COST every cent she had, since she'd neglected to bring her bank card with her, but now she appreciated her grandmother's old-fashioned notion of mad money—money to be used if a lady got mad and had to find her own way home. It had seemed so stupid on her few dates in high school. It didn't seem nearly so stupid now.

Sean had burned his last bridge, and she had a pretty good notion that, due to her parting words, so had she.

Good.

Ghengis, the most dependable man in her life, was waiting on the windowsill when she arrived home, and somehow sensing that she was not in the mood to put up with nonsense, he didn't even try to snag her mohair stole as usual.

She kicked her shoes off, pushed them under the coffee table, padded barefoot into the kitchen and went straight for the ice cream. She ate three big spoonfuls of toffee crunch before concluding that she was not about to let Sean Nielsen ruin her life and her waistline.

GABE HAD LEFT REHAB. Again. Tony had tried to call the hospital to find out if they would let him talk to Gabe—

although Gabe had not spoken to him voluntarily in months—and had been informed that Gabe was no longer a patient at their facility.

He was probably with Val, Tony decided after hanging up the phone and going to sit on the bed with his back against the wall. It made sense, since Val hadn't phoned him, frantic. And whenever Gabe came out of rehab—even after the short stints—he was usually pretty good for a while. Tony sincerely hoped that this time it would be for a long while.

Mutt crossed the room to put his head in Tony's lap and Tony absently stroked the dog's ears.

He stared sightlessly across the room for a long time before blowing out a frustrated breath. If he hadn't pushed Gabe to follow him into undercover work, the guy would probably be sitting in a patrol car right now. Happy as hell. Tony rubbed a hand over his face wearily.

He hated the fact that he'd so totally screwed up a good friend's life.

TONY ORDERED HIS PIZZA from a shop a couple of miles away and, by tipping generously, had trained the delivery boy to go directly to his basement door—despite the kid's obvious concern about Muttzilla. Tony wanted to tell him that the cat was more of a danger, but didn't want to scare the boy off.

He heard Jasmine come home just before the pizza arrived—pretty early for her having been on a date. Her shoes had made sharp clicks on the floor above him for several minutes, and then she must have taken the shoes off, because he could still hear her moving, but not any more clicks.

Tony overtipped the pizza boy again, then flopped the box onto the old table in his room. He didn't open the lid.

He felt very alone, which was odd, since he rarely hung with other people. Normal, nonscumbag people, that is.

But there he was.

He was alone. Jasmine was alone. He wouldn't mind spending a little time with her, since it always made him feel…well, good, even though he didn't usually plan on it making him feel good.

Decision made.

He headed up the basement steps, tapping on the door when he reached the top. A few seconds passed before Jasmine responded.

"Hi," she said, pulling open the door and holding on to it so that he couldn't get past her. He wondered if it was accidental or purposeful. Or if Sean was there.

"Hi. I have extra pizza, if you'd like some." It wasn't difficult to see that Jasmine wasn't in the mood for company. "If you give me a plate, I'll bring some up for you," he said, abandoning his plan for a shared dinner.

"Peace offering?"

"Have I been bad?"

She smiled then, wearily. "I'm sure you have been at some point." She stepped back. "Maybe you could bring the entire pizza up here and we could share."

"We could." *Score.*

"I'll get the plates—you get the pizza." She turned and walked across the kitchen, and Tony couldn't help but admire how she looked in that black dress and her stocking feet. He also wondered what had happened to bring her home so early and put that expression on her face.

That guy she was dating, no doubt.

"So how was your day?" Jasmine asked a few minutes later as they were seated on opposite sides of her well-polished table.

Tony almost choked as he took his first bite of pizza.

"What?" she asked, perplexed.

"I don't know if I've ever had anyone say that to me over a dinner table." Didn't know if he was ready to have someone say such a thing to him. He might be up here having pizza with a woman he kind of had a crush on, but domestic harmony was just a wee bit too scary for him.

Jasmine was frowning at him, her pizza poised in the air. "I don't follow."

"How was your day, honey?" He did a pretty good imitation of a perky 1960s housewife.

"So," Jasmine said ironically, "how *was* your day? Honey?"

"Swell. Sun on my back. Earth on my hands."

"Very poetic."

"You could do my ego a favor and not act so surprised that I can be poetic."

"I'm not surprised. I'm just…" She gestured with her free hand.

"Surprised."

"I was surprised to see you with Mrs. Thorpe." She took a bite of pizza, pulling the cheese with her teeth in a rather unladylike way that Tony appreciated.

"You saw us?"

She nodded after she swallowed. "I did, but I didn't want to disturb you. You were busy."

"I learned some important stuff, and if Mutt behaves himself, you might have some nice perennials."

"You better be careful, Tony."

He cocked his head. "Why's that?"

"You sound like you're on the edge of being domesticated."

He snorted, which he hoped covered the fact that she'd unnerved him, and reached for another slice of pizza. "It won't take."

"How do you know?"

"It hasn't yet."

"How many people have tried?"

"Not that many," he said truthfully. He tended to hang out with the fast, undomesticated crowd. "So what do you tame people do after pizza?"

"We crochet. Or watch videos. Or read." She twirled a bit of cheese around her finger, then popped it into her mouth.

"Sounds…mind numbing." And pretty similar to what he did after pizza—except for the video and crocheting part.

"I can probably dig up an extra crochet hook."

"I can probably go back downstairs."

"Please don't."

He shot her a quick look. The urgency in the simple statement was unexpected. "Why?"

She shrugged with studied nonchalance, possibly a little surprised herself. "I guess because I'm enjoying having some company." She wadded her napkin up and set it on the table, obviously done after two slices, whereas Tony was still warming up. "And I had a rotten evening. I thought I wanted to be alone and—" one corner of her mouth quirked up "—you know, sulk? But then you showed up and I like this better."

Okay, did he ask about the evening? Not ask? If he wasn't attracted to her, he'd ask in a heartbeat. *What happened to make things rotten?* But then, before he could decide what to do, she sidetracked him by saying, "Why *did* you show up, anyway?"

Caught.

"I had extra pizza."

"I'm certain that's happened before and you just put it in your minifridge."

She had him there. And he felt as though he was on the verge of squirming uncomfortably. This was crazy. He'd dated some pretty forward women in his time—including a lap dancer named Poison Ivy—and hadn't had any trouble holding his own. But that was because he understood them. He was still working on understanding Jasmine.

He decided to come clean. "I wanted company."

She smiled then, in a way that made his breath catch. How could he have ever thought her driver's license photo was prettier than she was in the flesh?

"Let's move the pizza into the living room. I promise, no crocheting."

He hesitated. "I didn't mean to elbow my way into your evening." And in a strange way, he now hoped she'd send him back downstairs. Where it was safe.

She simply picked up the pizza box and walked into the living room, where the giant cat was draped across the back of an easy chair, eyeing Tony malevolently as he followed with the beverages.

"Behave, Ghengis."

The cat twitched his tail when Jasmine spoke, then closed his eyes—but Tony had a feeling, as he settled on the sofa, that the cat was still watching him through tiny slits.

Good. He'd have an incentive to keep things on the up-and-up. Didn't want that big cat attacking him the way he'd attacked Mutt and the guy in the garage.

TONY MIGHT HAVE WANTED company, but he was on edge. Avoiding her eyes, not being his usual flippant self. Finally Jasmine took the matter in hand, after he'd closed the pizza box and drained his glass of water.

"Why'd you need company *tonight,* Tony?" she asked quietly. "Did something happen?"

He hesitated for long enough that it appeared as if he was picking one reason out of many, and that made her heart twist a little. "I got some bad news about a friend," he said.

He didn't elaborate and Jasmine didn't push. They sat regarding each other for another moment, and she fully expected him to jump to his feet and call it a night.

"Now you tell me something. Why are you so organized?"

She laughed because it was so not a topic she'd thought he'd bring up. "Control," she said, finding it easier to admit than she'd thought it would be.

"Control."

"Yes. I know that ultimately I can't control life, but...I feel better trying to control the things I can, so I do it."

"Why does it make you feel better?"

She rubbed her hands over her temples, smoothing her hair behind her ears. "The million-dollar question, eh? Probably because the more I control things, the less likely it'll be that the unexpected will happen."

"Don't like the unexpected?"

"Not much," she admitted. She lifted her chin, stared off across the room, thinking maybe she didn't like being analyzed all that much, either. Tony didn't take the hint.

"Why?" The tips of his fingers came to rest on her shoulder, making her nerves jump.

"Okay, this isn't logical."

"I'm prepared," he said gravely.

She wished she were. She was never good talking about this, even though so much time had passed. "My mom died unexpectedly when I was six. She had an aneurysm."

"That's a nasty bit of unexpected." Tony's eyes were dark and solemn. Understanding.

She pulled in a shaky breath. "The worst. And even though I know organization and control don't protect me from things like that…well—" she smiled philosophically at him "—the illusion comforts me." *And it had helped her deal with her perfectionist father while growing up. Two birds, one stone.*

"Must be why you enjoy what's-his-name's company."

"In the beginning, yes. He was a good fit."

"And now?"

"Not such a good fit." And that was all she was saying on the matter of *what's his name*. Tony didn't press for details. In fact, he didn't say anything.

Neither did Jasmine. She didn't move, and she didn't smile. She just…studied him, cataloging the things she found attractive about him—things she hadn't allowed herself to dwell on while she'd been dating Sean and ignoring gut instinct. His dark eyes, firm mouth. His most excellent cheekbones. That mop of curls. Her first impression of him was definitely not her current one.

She must have been telegraphing, because his eyes narrowed a bit. She could see him debating, and decided to help him out as he weighed his decision. It was so easy to reach out and take his hand, interlace their fingers...tip those scales.

Their hands stayed linked for only a few seconds before he released her fingers to gently pull her onto his lap. His arms were warm and solid as they closed around her. She nestled against him, finding his lips as if it were the most natural thing in the world.

Oh, but he kissed sweetly. Somehow she'd assumed that he'd be more forceful, aggressive. She hadn't expected his mouth to be so warm, so welcoming, his touch so light. She hadn't expected to want to melt into him so completely. She wanted to ask him if he was always this gentle, but hesitated to break the spell.

So Tony had to do it.

"Is this something else you tame people do?" he asked when they finally came up for air.

"I think this is what everyone does." She nuzzled his lower lip as she spoke, felt his response. She longed to keep doing it, but suddenly had this very bad feeling that she was doing it for all the wrong reasons. She was upset with Sean, seeking comfort. Maybe even using Tony...

Not a good thing. She pulled back a little. Tony picked up the cue.

"It's getting late," he said.

"Yes."

"I should go downstairs."

No doubt. She eased herself off his lap, smoothed her hair back from her forehead with both hands after she stood, felt a little guilty when she realized she'd rather be running her hands over him, regardless of her motivation.

"That was fun," Tony said at the basement door, his tone purposely light. "Probably won't happen again, will it?"

He was laying ground rules, and Jasmine was going to accept them. For now, anyway. Until she figured some things out.

"Probably not," she said with a half smile.

"Friends?"

"Friends." What else could they be realistically? But she was surprised to find that messing on the edge of danger—something she'd never really done— *had* been fun.

He paused to kiss her forehead before going down the steps, and that was that.

Jasmine closed the door and turned to lean against it. A few seconds went by before she realized she was still smiling.

She walked across the kitchen feeling amazingly…free.

Too bad perfect nine-to-five Sean, who wasn't going off to chase bad guys because it was the only life he knew, couldn't have a few more of Tony's easygoing characteristics.

WELL, HE'D KISSED THE landlady and hadn't got tossed out on his ear. Mainly because she'd invited him to kiss her. Jasmine was starting to emerge from her shell, and he didn't know if that was a good thing—at least, not with him involved.

Tony shrugged out of his shirt, then stood for moment,

reflecting on what had just occurred, before wadding the shirt and shoving it deep into his laundry bag.

He hadn't exactly *planned* for pizza night to end the way it did, but he'd done just about everything he could to make certain it did—dinner, hanging around afterward like a lonely teenage boy.

Shit.

Well, no harm done. Jasmine had had a fight with her beau and was working things out. Tony was handy, and frankly, he was kind of glad he could be there to help.

Otherwise how would he have discovered that Jasmine did not kiss like a librarian?

Now he just had to shove the whole incident out of his mind and make certain it didn't happen again. Jasmine's life wasn't perfect, but it was certainly more perfect without him than it would be with him.

TONY WAS GETTING TIRED of being jerked out of a deep sleep by the telephone. He fumbled on the nightstand for his cell phone, then sat up as he saw the number.

Yates.

But it wasn't Yates. It was Melanie, looking for her husband.

"He's not here."

"But…" He could hear a note of stubbornness in her voice when she asked, "Has he told you anything? I mean…darn it, Tony, he's probably off watching a house somewhere, searching for Davenport."

More likely looking for probable cause.

"Honest, Melanie. He hasn't told me a thing. If he's not home in an hour, call me."

And then Tony flopped onto his back and stared at the ceiling. Was Yates out hunting for Davenport because of the subtle threat to Melanie? Damn.

He rolled out of bed and was reaching for his pants, when the phone rang again.

"He's here," Melanie said in a low voice. "I'm sorry I bothered you."

"No problem. I understand."

And he *did* understand, since as a kid he'd waited up for his mom more times than she knew.

ANDY POKED HIS HEAD into Jasmine's cubicle, where she was in the middle of processing book requests. "Someone here to see you."

Jasmine was half-afraid it was Sean, but when she exited the library office, it was Georgia of all people, standing on the other side of the big wooden checkout counter.

"So what happened?" she said as she set an oversize book on the counter.

Jasmine automatically scanned the bar code on the book before chancing a guess at what she meant. "At the theater?"

"Yes, at the theater. I mean, you show up with the hunk and then he spends the performance alone."

"I went home with a headache," Jasmine said.

Georgia laughed. "He looked like he had a headache, too. And when I told Melanie about it, she was curious why you live with Tony but go to the theater with some other guy. I told her you librarians live life hard." She laughed at her joke and Jasmine was glad she wasn't close enough to get poked in the ribs.

"I don't like to tie myself down," she said drily, and Georgia laughed again.

"Why don't you come to my birthday party this Saturday. Bring one of your guys."

"I have a function I have to attend. It's kind of important." Her relationship with her father might not be the best, but he was her dad, for better, for worse, and she would be there when he was honored.

"That's too bad. Well, if you get done early, we'll be at a place called No Regrets. It's on Fourth Street."

"I'll keep that in mind." Even though she seriously doubted she'd be attending, she wouldn't hurt Georgia's feelings.

"Do that."

JASMINE'S FATHER'S FLIGHT had been delayed, so he'd called to say he'd be flying into Seattle a few hours before the presentation. He would barely have time to make the ceremony, and then he would be flying out the next day.

"Maybe we can have breakfast," Jasmine had said on a sigh. For some reason, she never gave up trying to play the game. "Before tomorrow's flight."

He shocked her by saying, "I was planning on that."

"Good," Jasmine said. "Oh…I guess I should tell you…things didn't work out with Sean Nielsen. He won't be attending the reception with me."

The silence that followed brought back memories of other times she hadn't managed to live up to expectations. Finally, her father said in a cool tone, "Perhaps you can find someone to bring in his place. There'll be an empty chair at our table."

"I'll try to find someone."

Jasmine slowly hung up the phone. She loved her father, but she was getting darned tired of the feeling that she was just one big disappointment.

And now she had to dig up a date.

"YOU'RE ASKING ME TO go to a dress-up dinner," Tony spoke flatly. Disbelievingly.

"I did a favor for you and went bowling. Now you can do a favor for me." She was not backing down.

"But bowling is fun. And I don't have anything to wear."

"Yes, you do. I saw you in a suit jacket the other day."

"My court clothes?"

"I guess. They're fine." And she'd been to enough academic awards presentations to know that the people attending would be dressed in everything from fine wool and silk to corduroy and denim. There'd probably even be a few pairs of jeans present.

"Will you do me this favor or not?"

Tony leaned a hip against her counter. "Are you sure you want me?"

"Do you own clean clothes?" she asked with an air of finality.

"I live next to the washing machine."

"Then, yes, I want you." She was beginning to wonder if she might want him more than was appropriate.

He pushed off the counter. "All right. Since I have a good—what?—couple of hours before we leave, I guess I'll go fire up old Betsy and mow the grass. Like I was going to do before I was shanghaied."

Jasmine couldn't help smiling. "Thank you."

He sauntered out the door, Ghengis at his heels. The

cat rubbed his head against the dog's chest as he walked by. Muttzilla looked disgusted but didn't retaliate.

Jasmine shook her head and headed for her closet. She had to find something that went with corduroy.

CHAPTER ELEVEN

TONY WAS WEARING FINE WOOL when Jasmine answered the tap on her basement door and let him into the kitchen. He looked good and Jasmine suspected that he may have spent some of his hard-earned money on appropriate clothing when he'd disappeared that afternoon. She would have been happy with his court clothes, but instead, he'd shown up wearing dark charcoal slacks, a light gray sport coat, a white shirt and blue tie. And his hair—the curls weren't entirely tamed, but were on the verge of behaving. Jasmine speculated about what state they'd be in at the end of the evening. Personally, she liked them wild.

"You look nice," Jasmine said.

"I borrowed the coat and tie from Yates," he confessed. "But everything else is from the House of DeMonte."

"Very stylish."

He let his eyes travel over her, but he didn't say anything, making Jasmine wonder if he approved or disapproved of her artfully beaded dress, which not that long ago, wouldn't have mattered. Not that long ago she wouldn't have bought such a frivolous dress.

"Well?" She spread her hands wide, inviting a comment.

His eyes were warm when he said, "I think I like you in green."

THE AWARDS CEREMONY WAS slated to start at eight o'clock, and Jasmine's father had called at seven to tell her that he had indeed made it Mondell and would meet her at the reception.

It was dusk as she and Tony left in his small car. He'd even vacuumed it out for the occasion, which she appreciated since she was wearing silk, sworn enemy of Great Dane hair.

They took the back route to the university, driving through the older part of town. She'd noticed before that Tony was always on alert while driving, and tonight was no exception. He seemed aware of everything, even while they were carrying on a conversation. She supposed his being so alert had kept him alive all his forty-two years.

"Have you ever heard of a guy named Robert Davenport?" he asked as they passed an electronics warehouse.

"No. Should I have?"

"Probably not. He's making Yates crazy—" Tony abruptly stopped speaking, and a split second later, Jasmine saw why. A person dropped to the ground from a high window just inside the alley they were passing and took off at a dead run.

"Son of a bitch! It's *him*," Tony muttered as he jammed the car into Park and leaped out. "Call Dispatch. Number two, speed dial. Burglary suspect. And lock the doors."

Jasmine sat, mouth open, as Tony tore on down the alley after the runner, and then she fumbled for the phone he'd tossed on the seat. Number two, speed dial. The phone lit up.

"I'm, um, with an officer who just…took off on a

foot chase," she said as soon as the dispatcher came on the line. "We're in the alley behind the Cedar Lane Mall. He ran…west? He asked me to call Dispatch."

"Who is the officer?"

"Tony DeMonte."

"What is your name?"

"Jasmine Storm," she said impatiently. "Look, he needs some help."

Just as the words left her lips, she was astonished to see a runner cut back into the alley from a side street, a few blocks down from where both men had disappeared a few minutes earlier. The man was too short to be Tony, and he was running hell-bent for election. Tony might run every day, but he was not going to catch this guy.

Tony appeared then at least twenty yards behind the runner.

"They're coming back down the alley. Send help."

Jasmine slid the phone onto the dash, then grasped the door handle.

In a matter of seconds the runner was nearly at the car, which partially blocked the entrance to the alley. Jasmine breathed deeply, grasped the door handle and pushed the door open, directly into the runner's path. He hit the door with a solid thud that bounced it shut again. Jasmine recoiled in her seat, unnerved by the impact. The man reeled sideways for a few steps before regaining his footing and taking off, but Tony was on him by then. Jasmine opened the door again as soon as Tony had the guy on the ground—just in case he needed some kind of help.

"There's a flex cuff in the glove compartment," Tony said from between clenched teeth as he wrestled with the man. Jasmine opened the compartment just as head-lights turned into the alley.

"Never mind," Tony said as an officer got out of his patrol car.

Close to twenty minutes passed before the respond-ing officer got the story, inspected the door, told Tony a joke and then sent Jasmine and Tony on their way.

And while that was going on, Jasmine stood in the night air, her arms wrapped around her middle, as she stared at the big dent she'd put in Tony's door. He had his man, one he'd been trying to catch for some time ap-parently, but he was also going to need a body shop.

The minute the patrol car left the alley, Tony rounded on Jasmine with no sign of the jovial bonhomie he'd shared with the other officer.

"Are you crazy?"

"I'm sorry about the door. I'll pay for it."

"The hell you will. And you didn't answer my question."

"Am I crazy? That question?"

"Yes."

"I don't…" Her voice faded as she gave him a skep-tical look.

He put his hands on her shoulders. It was not a tender gesture. "You could have been hurt. Do you understand that?"

She nodded. "I didn't have time to think. It just seemed a logical way to stop the guy. I was going to lock the door after it shut again."

"What if he'd bent the frame and it couldn't shut?"

"I, uh…"

"Don't do things like that." He let go of her, shoved

his hand through his curls, sending them back to their natural state. "I mean, damn it, don't *do* things like that."

"All right," Jasmine said in a small voice.

"Let's go." He started for the car. Jasmine got in the passenger seat. They shut their doors, and then stared at each other for a long moment before simultaneously directing their gazes forward. Tony muttered as he jammed the key into the ignition.

"I'll drive you to the presentation—" he glanced down at his pants, with the alley stains on the knees and his scuffed-up shoes "—you might be better off going stag. I can wait for you."

Jasmine nodded and looked forward again. She'd fight this battle once they got there.

TONY WAS RELIEVED WHEN Jasmine nodded, but when he pulled up in front of the campus civic center, she said, "I would like it if you came in with me."

"No, you wouldn't."

She was getting that stubborn expression on her face. Damn, he was glad things had ended as they had, so he had a chance to watch her get that stubborn expression. She didn't understand how nuts some of those guys could get.

"Yes. I would."

"You are driving me crazy tonight."

"In a good way, I hope," she said with exaggerated primness.

"In the best way," he said sarcastically. The corners of his mouth tightened as he glanced again at his pants and shoes. "You sure about this?"

"Go into the restroom once we get inside, and take care of what you can."

"This is more than a little spit on a Kleenex can fix."

She smiled. "Did your mom used to do that?"

"All moms do that," he said, reaching for the door handle. Even his mom. It had to be in the handbook.

Tony never got a chance to fix things. As soon as they entered, someone directed Jasmine across the room to the head table and Tony followed, reminding himself that she'd taken him in off the street and saved him from Georgia. The least he could do was stick with her and pray that they were seated soon.

A man who bore an unmistakable resemblance to Jasmine stood as she approached the table.

"Hi, Dad," she said, giving him a rather stiff hug. "Did you have a good flight?"

"How good could it be when it was so damn late?"

"Good enough to get you here," Jasmine replied mildly, and her father appeared a bit surprised before he directed his attention to Tony, who held out a hand.

"Tony DeMonte," he said before Jasmine had a chance to perform introductions.

"Richard Storm." From the frosty expression on his face, it was safe to assume that Richard Storm was none too impressed with Tony DeMonte.

More introductions followed, and Tony found that he would be sitting with two CEOs, an economics theorist and the dean of the Mondell University Business College, along with various spouses—two of which were now surreptitiously inspecting his scarred-up trousers, because for some reason no one was sitting. Everyone remained standing, chatting politely, taking turns staring at his pants.

Yes, he was going to be a real conversation piece. He

was certain that Jasmine wasn't regretting her decision to have him come in with her.

"Tony made an arrest on the way over," Jasmine announced casually when the third person in the group did a veiled double take at his legs.

"An arrest?" her father said.

"Tony's a police officer." Jasmine sipped from the glass of water she was holding.

"Who did you arrest?" the dean's wife asked.

"A suspected burglar. There've been a number of burglaries in the area, so I couldn't let the opportunity pass."

He smiled crookedly and the dean's wife smiled back before turning to Jasmine. "And you were there for the arrest?"

"My very first."

"Tell us about it…"

Tony noticed Jasmine's father studying him as they dined, as if trying to identify genus and species, and he had to admit that the guy was putting him on edge. He was one cold man. Jasmine must have gotten her warmth from her mother. Or whoever had raised her.

The dinner progressed through the courses. Then the table was cleared, speeches were made and Mr. Storm was presented with his award. More speeches. Coffee. Speeches. All punctuated by Mr. Storm giving him the freeze ray.

Jasmine reached under the table and touched Tony's hand at one point, startling him. And then she smiled and for a moment it was just the two of them—until Tony shook the moment off. There was no two of them—not in the sense he'd just been feeling.

WELL, THIS WAS GOING just great, Jasmine thought as she pushed her way into the ladies' room after the last round of speeches. She really should have gone with Tony to Georgia's birthday party—it would have been more fun for both of them. The only high point of the evening was watching Sean across the room, obviously fuming because the cop in the basement was at the honoree's table and he was not.

Everyone at that table seemed to find Tony fascinating, including the dean's wife, who had looked as if she wanted to climb onto his lap after the second cocktail. Everyone except for her father, that is, who was behaving like a frigidly polite ass, in Jasmine's estimation. She wouldn't have asked Tony to escort her if she'd realized he'd get snubbed by the guest of honor. She was, for once in her life, going to say something about it when they went to breakfast the next morning.

As luck would have it, though, she bumped into her father, who was also returning to the table.

"That's an interesting date you brought," he said in a low voice as they walked along the periphery of the room. He smiled and nodded at an acquaintance.

"Interesting?" Jasmine echoed. "How so?"

"Well…I didn't expect you to bring a scruffy cop with stained pants when I asked you to fill the chair." His voice was little more than a whisper, but it stopped Jasmine dead.

"Tony is not scruffy," she said carefully, her voice barely above a whisper. "And he ruined his pants in the line of duty."

Her father's eyebrows rose as they always did when

he was challenged. "That's admirable, but couldn't you have chosen someone a little less conspicuous to sit at our table?"

Jasmine pressed her lips together. Counted to ten. It did no good. Thankfully, no one was near, so she was able to say what was on her mind—what had *been* on her mind for years.

"Dad. I've spent my life trying to live up to your expectations, yet you have put very little effort into living up to mine."

He frowned deeply, obviously startled by her blunt statement. "Excuse me?"

"*My* expectations. I'm part of this equation, too, and I expect you to take an interest in my life. To give me some moral support and…well, to understand when my date has to arrest someone on the way to a function."

"Jasmine, that is not funny, and this is neither the time nor place for this ridiculous conversation."

"True." She turned on her heel. He caught up with her in a few steps. "Where are you going?"

"To rescue my date."

An admirer came bearing down on them then, beaming as he held his hand out to her father, and Jasmine took advantage of the moment to make her escape.

She headed straight for Tony, who'd been eyeing them from the table, his expression carefully blank. Being a police officer, he'd probably deduced that the exchange had not been positive, but Jasmine did not want him to know that his presence had sparked it. She just wanted out of there. She was *not* about to go home and stew, and she couldn't think of any better place to go and not stew than at Georgia's party. She had never in her life been to a party in a bar. It was time.

"Is everything all right?" Tony asked in a tone that reinforced her belief he could read lips and knew exactly what had transpired between her and her father.

"Absolutely fine," she said in a flat voice. "How do you feel about attending a birthday party?"

Tony frowned. "Will there be speeches?"

"Not one."

He got out of his chair, nodded at the remaining guests as he put his hand under her elbow. "Let's go."

THERE WAS A GOOD-SIZE crowd at No Regrets—the ambulance crews that weren't on call, a few firefighters, a few cops—including Bill.

"Jasmine!"

Georgia pushed her way through the crowd just as Tony took possession of the pitcher of beer he'd ordered at the bar. She hugged Jasmine as though she'd known her forever. "I'm glad you could make it. Hey, Tony."

"Hi."

"Get in a fight or something?" Georgia asked, eyeing his pants. "That must have been some function." And then she spotted another arrival and hurried off toward the door.

Tony escorted Jasmine to the one unoccupied table, pulled out her chair after setting down the pitcher and glasses. She tried to smile as Tony sat beside her, his hand still on the back of her chair, but he was aware she was still gnawing on the incident at the reception.

She wasn't having a lot of luck with the men in her

life lately—and she wasn't willing to talk about what had transpired with her father. He'd asked a couple of safe questions on the drive over to give her an opening, but she hadn't bitten. She muttered once or twice, and he soon realized she was more angry than hurt. That was a good sign. Angry he could deal with. Hurt required more finesse, and he was rusty in the finesse department.

He poured beer for both of them, waited to see if she was going to say anything.

"Thank you for escorting me tonight," she finally said. Her tone was still slightly stony, as was her expression. "My dad is kind of a…"

He thought she was going to say *tight-ass,* which had been his personal assessment.

"Difficult man to deal with sometimes. I'm sorry he was rude to you tonight."

Tony laughed. "You're talking to a guy who makes traffic stops."

"He drives me crazy," Jasmine said on a sigh. "I love him, but… Never mind."

"It's okay if you need to unload. It won't go any further."

"I don't need to unload. I already did that. To him."

"First time?"

"First time out loud." She lifted her glass and sniffed the contents, making Tony wonder if he should have poured for her without asking.

"Do you drink beer? Because I can get you something else…"

She raised a hand. "No. Beer is fine."

Melanie and Yates came through the door. Georgia broke through the crowd to meet them.

"Is it going to be okay?" he asked when he focused back on Jasmine.

"Between me and Dad? I'm sure it will be," she said, at last lifting the glass to her lips and sipping. "Once he realizes I'm right. So…ten, twelve years and we're good."

Tony smiled, touched her hand lightly with his fingertips.

Stop touching her.

Easier said than done. She was so damned pretty. He had to get a grip. This was not a woman to be chasing, messing with—especially when he knew how great she kissed, how nicely their bodies snuggled together.

"Did you ever stop to think that a guy like your father might not have been prepared to raise a little girl on his own?"

"It has crossed my mind," she said, now cupping the glass in both hands, unaware that she was warming the contents. "But trust me, he could have made more of an effort." She took another sip.

"Jasmine, do you play shuffleboard?" Georgia bellowed from a few feet away.

"A little." Which probably meant she was a master, Tony surmised from the bowling and softball experiences.

"Bill doesn't have a partner."

Jasmine didn't seem to drink that much as the night progressed, but what she did drink apparently went right to her head, because for the first time since he'd met her, Jasmine allowed herself to cut loose. Not much by Tony's standards, but for Jasmine, it was a big step.

Tony watched as she played shuffleboard in her fancy green beaded dress, then shot an adequate game of pool.

He stayed close enough that when the ambulance guys ogled her, they were aware of him, too.

"Did you take a pool-shooting class?" he asked after her game.

Jasmine smiled up at him, and once again he had that only-the-two-of-them feeling. But this time he didn't look away. It was as if he couldn't help himself. He wanted to be close to her.

"Billiards and Bowling. Nine weeks of each and a written test at the end." There was laughter in her eyes, but by this time he wasn't focusing so much on her eyes as her mouth.

Which curved slightly. All he had to do was lean just a little and— His cell phone started buzzing.

He yanked it out of his pocket, checked the number. Val.

"I have to get this."

Jasmine smiled resignedly, and he stepped out the front door to the relative quiet of the street before answering.

"Well, they found him," Val said, not bothering to say hello.

"Where, and what kind of shape is he in?" Tony yanked his tie with one hand, half expecting to hear the worst. He hadn't realized that Gabe wasn't with Val.

"Spokane and he's in jail." A brief silence followed, during which Tony let out a long low breath of relief, before she said, "I'm going to leave him there."

"Val—" He broke off. It wasn't his place to give her advice. He was just glad Gabe hadn't ended up dead in an alley somewhere.

"I didn't sign on for martyrdom when I got married. I'm done."

Tony put one hand on the rough brick of the building,

dropped his head as he tried to figure out what to say to the justifiably disgruntled wife of an addict, then pushed off again as a group of people charged down the sidewalk.

After a moment of dead air, Val said, "When are you coming back to Seattle?"

"Not sure." He paced around the corner to the alley, slipping into the darkness.

"Can I see you?"

Something in her tone instantly put him on edge. "Why?"

"So I don't have to be alone."

He couldn't believe, after she'd walked out on him, that she was saying this. "I don't know how wise that would be."

"Yeah?" Her voice was husky as she asked, "Why not?"

He didn't answer.

"It doesn't have to be right away, but…we have some unfinished business."

Any business they'd had, she'd finished long ago. And she was hurting right now—not thinking all that straight.

"Are you alone?" he asked gruffly.

"Very."

She was missing the point. "Call your sister. Get her over there."

"Tony, sometimes you are such a son of a bitch."

He hadn't meant to be. It just happened. Tony rubbed his forehead with his wrist. He also remembered a time when Val hadn't even said words like that.

"And you owe me."

His mouth compressed, but he didn't reply. Instead, he focused on the dimly lit brick wall across the alley with the green spray-painted graffiti, as Val continued.

"All those nights you went out drinking, partying, doping."

"It was part of the job, Val," he said. And he'd never done more than drink, unless he'd been in a serious situation. Then he faked if he could. Gabe had quit faking early on.

Not a hell of a lot Tony could have done about it. He'd actually tried, but Gabe hadn't bought.

"He had a problem. You should have done something instead of encouraging him."

Tony pinched the bridge of his nose. "All right, I'm responsible. You aren't going to leave him in jail, are you?"

He heard Val breathe deeply. "I don't know." And then she hung up.

Tony stared at his phone for a moment before dialing Dispatch. He got the number for the Spokane County sheriff's department and called. He hung up a few minutes later, assured that his former partner was doing as well as could be expected and that unless someone stepped forward to pay his bond, he'd be in the tank for a while for driving under the influence of a controlled substance.

Gabe was in jail and Tony was about to go back to a birthday party.

The bar was even more crowded when Tony went inside, and it took him a few minutes to find Jasmine in the corner near the pool table, "talking" with one of the ambulance guys who'd had more than his legal limit.

"You're *really* a librarian?" the guy asked as he leaned in toward her, barely keeping his balance.

"Yes," Jasmine said with a tight back-off-buddy smile.

"You don't look like a librarian," Mr. Ambulance Driver persisted, not taking the hint. Jasmine appeared to be on the verge of decking him if he didn't cease and desist. Tony decided to rescue the guy.

"She is a librarian," Tony said, edging past him to grab Jasmine's hand and lead her away.

"I could have handled that," Jasmine said as they skirted the crowded room, their fingers still loosely linked. Someone had managed to crank up the volume on the stereo system and the place was literally rocking.

"No doubt, but this was quick and easy," Tony said, his hand tightening on hers. He stopped. There was a sheen of perspiration across her forehead from the heat of many bodies packed closely together and the music was starting to get to him. "Call it a night?" he asked. He would stay if she wanted to, but after his chat with Val, he wouldn't be great company.

"Sure," Jasmine said. But instead of walking toward the exit, she brushed his cheek with her palm. He felt the simple caress down to his toes.

She smiled sweetly up at him. "You've gone beyond the call of escort duty. Let's go home."

THE NIGHT AIR WAS crisp and smelled faintly of burning leaves, a nice change from the beer-soaked atmosphere they'd just left, but Tony didn't seem to notice as he walked Jasmine up to her door. He'd been preoccupied for most of the drive home, although he'd made a few minor stabs at small talk.

"Thanks for tonight," Jasmine said after digging her keys out of her purse. "And by the way, I am paying for your door."

That got his attention. "Are not."

"Try to stop me."

He dropped his chin to his chest, blowing out a long breath in an exaggerated expression of frustration.

She smiled, glad to see the old Tony back. "You want to come in?"

He lifted his head. "Better not."

It wasn't what he said but how he said it that made her reply, "I wasn't inviting you into my bed." Not directly anyway. "We have an agreement, after all."

He looked at her in a way that made her nerves tingle. "Sometimes things don't work out as we intend them to."

She raised her eyebrows. "You sound pretty sure of that."

"I'm pretty sure we have some chemistry."

She couldn't argue that. She felt it. In spades.

"Obviously," she said, fitting her key into the lock. Ghengis marched out onto the porch, ears back, and she hefted him into her arms. His body was stiff and un-yielding, which made carrying him all the more diffi-cult, but tonight wasn't his turn to be outside.

Normally, Jasmine would have been tucking tail and running by this time, but instead, she drew herself up and asked, "Why can't we just…" she couldn't believe she was actually saying this, out loud, no less "…play around with the chemistry?"

Tony seemed to mentally step back, but his voice was gentle when he said, "Because—no offense—you're edging past tipsy to will-regret-this-in-the cold-light-of-morning. How's that for a reason?"

She was surprised to find that she could smile. "What else you got?"

"How about the truth."

The smile slowly faded from her lips. "What's the truth, Tony?"

"The truth is that I don't want to start something, all right?" She tilted her chin, silently indicating that he should continue. "I'm not the kind of guy you need to have mucking up your nice orderly life. It's best to just leave things as they are. Simple and uncomplicated."

She opened her mouth to argue, but he took her by the shoulders, turned her around, cat and all, and gave her a gentle push toward the door. "Go to bed, Jasmine. I'll see you in the morning, when you've had a chance to sleep this off and be grateful that one of us was thinking straight."

She went into the house without further protest, letting him shut the door. "He's wrong," she told the cat as she set him down. She wasn't all that tipsy and she really wished Tony had come in.

And she really wished the switch plates in her house would stay in place. This time she wasn't calling Tony. She got the screwdriver, fit the loosened screw into the hole of the electrical plate next to her kitchen stove and tightened it.

Maybe she had poltergeists. Or gremlins. At this point, she was beyond caring.

CHAPTER TWELVE

TONY STOOD IN HIS BOXERS, massaging his forehead after peeling out of his clothing. Hell of a night. The hardest part had been shutting Jasmine down.

He folded Yates's stuff so that he could have it cleaned, shoved the rest into his laundry bag. Truth to tell, he wished for nothing more than to take Jasmine into her bed and make love to her for the rest of the night. And most of the next day.

He was pretty much falling for her, which was why it was so important that he not do that stuff. This was new territory, nothing like what he'd experienced with Val. That had been good—until she'd blindsided him by leaving him for Gabe—but this…this had a whole different feel to it.

It scared him.

Other cops had relationships, which rarely panned out because of job stress. And his cop job was more intense than most. Plus his life was…less organized than Jasmine could handle. Hell, he was broke. Jasmine was tougher than she looked, but why put her through the pain if he didn't have to?

He wouldn't go off the deep end, as Gabe had—he would have done it long ago if so—but he didn't want to hurt Jasmine the way his mother had hurt his father, or the way Yates was hurting Melanie even though he loved her. And he wasn't exactly in a position to quit his job and start something new, when he was supporting both himself and his mom. Not when he was only ten years from a fairly decent retirement.

Besides, he was used to being alone. He'd probably spend the remainder of his professional life alone.

"Got it?" he asked himself out loud, attempting to beat the concept into his thick skull, or maybe to convince his libido to back off. "Alone. All by yourself."

Mutt raised his head, studying Tony through sad eyes.

"Except for you," Tony said as he sank onto the bed, resting his forearms on his bare thighs and clasping his hands loosely together as he regarded his only companion.

The dog thumped his tail once and closed his eyes.

TONY MADE HIMSELF scarce the next day, which didn't surprise Jasmine after what had transpired last night on her porch. The librarian coming on to the big, bad, rapidly backpedaling cop would almost have been amusing—if she hadn't failed so miserably.

She'd certainly hung herself out there—something she never, ever did. But she'd done it last night.

And she wasn't sorry. Maybe a lingering effect of her confrontation with her father, who hadn't called about breakfast and should be on his flight back to California about now. He'd be in contact eventually. She hoped. If not, she'd fix things later, after they'd both had some time to stew—and their relationship was *not* going back to the way it was.

She was tired of trying to live the perfect, controlled life. Being in control hadn't saved her mother, and it wouldn't save her or make her the perfect daughter, regardless of how many years she had labored under that illusion. In fact, last night had taught her that she liked to shake things up.

Logic and safety were good, but dating Sean *had* been logical and that hadn't turned out. Also, upon reflection, she did not believe for a moment that Sean hadn't known she was Richard Storm's daughter when he'd first approached her in that gallery weeks ago.

She'd watched him and one of his associates pointing out people to each other at the dinner. Without a doubt she'd been identified somewhere and then he had gone into action. Tony might not be as smooth as Sean, but he was a heck of a lot more honest.

Jasmine pushed the crochet hook deep into the ball of thread and then put the curtain panel aside. She had to go to the market, and then she'd tackle the other unsettling issue in her life. Whether Tony believed her or not, something strange was happening in her house. She felt it. She just couldn't prove it. So she'd speak to Mrs. Thorpe and her other neighbors to find out if anyone had noticed anything odd around her house. Surely someone had seen something.

As it turned out, no one had seen anything and two of her neighbors even mentioned that they'd answered similar questions from the police not all that long ago.

Mrs. Thorpe, who seemed much less distant now that she and Tony had bonded over bedding plants, reported that the meter reader and the postman, both people she recognized, made regular visits to Jasmine's house, but other than that, she hadn't observed any unusual activity.

However, she was also careful to point out that her windows were not situated so that she could see the entrance to Tony's quarters and she didn't have a clear view of the entire back porch unless she was on her own back porch...and leaned over the railing.

Jasmine thanked her and returned home, feeling better until she realized that Mrs. Thorpe, who had the best view of all, hadn't seen the man who'd secreted himself in the garage, either. And the lady also did volunteer work on a regular basis. It wouldn't be that difficult to figure out her schedule, as well as Jasmine's. And Tony's...

That was a lot of schedules. Jasmine was beginning to feel like the crazy cat lady again.

TONY'S CAR WAS GONE when she got home from work the next day, but Mutt was in the yard, lying under the tree, with Ghengis lying beside him. Jasmine blinked. Yes, they were together and no fur was flying. In fact, they looked quite contented, snoozing together in the shade.

She hoped Tony had seen them and taken note. Opposites not only attracted—they could get along well.

Inside the cool house, she dropped her tote by the door instead of carefully stowing it in the closet as usual, and went to make dinner. She felt like cooking something messy. It would keep her hands busy and give her something to think about other than the fact that she wanted something that she had no idea how to get. Tony. So did she let things lie for a while? Make another move?

That idea froze her up slightly, but…she'd survived the last time, hadn't she?

With the help of Budweiser. She probably wouldn't be following that route again, although it had been an interesting one.

Small particles of ashlike debris were scattered over the stove top. She frowned at the sight, then glanced up at the decorative metal plate that covered the hole where, a few decades ago, a stovepipe had once joined the chimney. It was in place. The gusts of wind earlier in the day must have forced air down the pipe and ash out from behind the plate.

Or the electrical cover plate gremlin was now messing with her chimney.

At least she didn't have squirrels, which Dorothy had contended with earlier in the year. She preferred gremlins and poltergeists to rodents any day. She wiped the ash off the stove with a cloth and then put the kettle on to boil her lasagna noodles. She'd eat what she could and bring the rest to Chad and Andy tomorrow.

THE SAUCE WAS BUBBLING in the pan and the water was just about to boil, when there was knock on the door.

Tony. And he was not looking friendly. The term "all business" sprang to mind.

Jasmine held the door wide, wondering what was up. "I didn't know you were working today."

"I got called in." He set a manila folder on the table, before glancing over at the tomato sauce simmering on the stove.

"We apprehended a guy today who was hiding on a woman's back porch. He knocked her down as he ran off."

Jasmine put her hand to her chest. "Is she all right?"

"No black eye," he said with a distant smile, "but scared, as you can imagine. Anyway, we picked the guy up not long afterward and he had a burglar kit on him."

"Do you think he's *my* guy?"

"Could be. Can I show you a photo lineup?" He reached into his folder.

"Why not." She'd failed miserably on the last one, which she'd examined within hours of her assault, but maybe something would stick out this time.

He carefully laid the photos out on the table. Jasmine peered at each one, hoping to feel some twinge of recognition, but she hadn't seen her assailant's face. She shook her head.

"You don't have any kind of a leaning toward any of them?"

"No."

He gathered the photos.

"Which one was it?"

"I can't say right now."

Jasmine lifted the tea bag out of her cup and set it on a saucer. "Even if this guy isn't my guy—" she pursed her lips thoughtfully "—my guy's not coming back, is he?"

"I'd be surprised. I think you put a scare into him."

Jasmine nodded. There was a brief, rather uncomfortable silence, before Tony walked over to the stove. He lifted the spoon out of her sauce, tasted and made a face.

"What is this?"

"It's tomato sauce."

"You need a new recipe."

"I didn't make it."

"Not canned sauce!"

She folded her arms over her chest. "Don't tell me the king of takeout is going to lecture me on prepared foods."

"No." He picked up the package of lasagna noodles. "But some things, if you're going to do them, you just have to do them right."

"Is lasagna one of those things, Tony?"

"Yes. Lasagna would be one of them."

"So…what do I do?"

"Where's your recipe?"

Jasmine pointed at the pasta package and Tony grimaced again.

"You're a real snob," she said. "You know that, don't you?"

"Can't help it." He started pushing up his shirt-sleeves. "I'm Italian."

"What are you doing?"

"Rescuing you from yourself."

"Aren't you on duty?"

He smiled with the air of man who was not going to be sidetracked. "Nope. They let me bring copies of the photos home. I'll return them tomorrow."

"In that case…" Jasmine spread her hands "…have at it."

Tony selected the ingredients from Jasmine's cabinets, commenting on the good, the bad and the ugly.

"Never buy this small garlic. And only buy Italian tomatoes."

"Gotcha."

He put her to work chopping the vegetables while he opened cans of whole tomatoes. "What are you doing?" he asked a moment later. Jasmine glanced up.

"Chopping?"

"No. You are… I don't know what you're doing. Here…" He took the knife and began rapidly decimating the poor onion she'd been cutting so carefully.

Her eyebrows rose.

"Come here." She stepped in between him and the counter. He placed her hand on the knife. "Hold the tip, then just move the handle up and down. See?"

She leaned her head back against his chest as he demonstrated. "Mmm-hmm."

"This is serious, Jasmine."

"Yes, it is." Because she could feel his body reacting to her nearness. She leaned back a little more, enjoying the sensation. His arm closed around her waist.

"Why didn't we do this the other night?" she asked huskily.

"I wasn't hungry."

She turned in his arms. "I'm not going to ask you if you're hungry now, because I'm pretty sure I have the answer." The knife clunked down onto the counter.

"Uh, yeah." His hands slipped lower, down over her butt, but his touch was still light.

"And I'm definitely not tipsy."

"But I'm still afraid," he said softly, truthfully. "And I have to go."

She stepped back suddenly. "What's wrong with me, Tony? I mean…" She held her hands wide. "What?"

"There's nothing wrong with you, Jasmine." She could see that he meant it.

"Then perhaps you can tell me why you're giving my ego such a battering?"

"Women who live in the suburbs and make lists as a hobby do not belong with guys like *me. That's* what's wrong."

"What do you mean by *belong?*"

"I mean *to be with.*"

"Why can't I be with you? Are you of the opinion I'm incapable of—" she felt a blush start to rise and attempted to battle it down by tossing her head carelessly "—*being with* you without needing all kinds of other things?"

"What kind of other things?"

"Like a full-blown commitment? Do you think I can't just enjoy myself like other women? Is that what you think?"

"I don't know what I think," he said lowly.

"Give me some credit, okay?"

"I'm trying to do the right thing here, Jasmine."

"For who?"

"For you!" He took a few paces, then turned toward her again. "I am ten years from retirement, yet I have no money. I am going back undercover. It's a dangerous job. I have no social skills. I'm not a good guy to be taking up with."

"What else, Tony?"

"I'm not good at relationships. I don't think I can stick with one. Even with you."

And she didn't know if she wanted one. She wanted to cut loose and who better than Tony to cut loose with?

She considered what he said, her brown eyes ultraserious.

"Anything else?"

"No. That's pretty much it."

"You've laid it all out?"

"Yeah."

"Do you believe I'm an adult woman, capable of making my own decisions?" He nodded, and she cocked her head. "Do you remember what you pulled out of the washing machine drain a few weeks ago?"

"Vaguely," he said with an edge of stiffness to his voice.

"I'm wearing it." She let the words sink in and the mental image form before she asked matter-of-factly, "Want to see?"

His gaze became intense. "You aren't playing fair."

"What's not fair? I saw you in your underwear."

"Yeah, but my underwear is bigger than yours."

"Let's compare."

"Jasmine," he muttered as he surrendered and pulled her against him, "this is very unlibrarianlike behavior."

"Yes." Her mouth settled on his in a hot, very unlibrarianlike kiss. "Isn't it grand?"

JASMINE HAD TO FORCE herself not to hum at work the next day. Easier said than done. Elise was shopping for the perfect birthday present for Andy, who would turn twenty-six later that week.

"He likes history, but a history book seems so lame," Elise said as she flipped a catalog closed.

Library employee or not, Jasmine had to admit that a history book was not a romantic birthday present.

"Maybe later in the relationship."

"You mean when things are more boring?"

"Exactly."

"Get him a metal detector," Chad said as he walked by. Elise scowled at him. "Oh, yes. The perfect small gift. I was thinking of something that would allow me to buy groceries for the rest of the month."

"Why a *metal* detector?" Jasmine asked.

"He's interested in prospecting," Chad said, wheeling a cart full of children's books out from behind the counter. "His dad used to do it—you know, up in those old mining claims in the mountains behind town. He's always pricing nuggets on the Internet when he's supposed to be cataloging."

Elise nodded. "He has mentioned those mines, but…I'll just steer away from the rock-related gifts."

"What else is he interested in?" Jasmine asked, accepting that maybe Chad might actually have some usable information.

"Historical buildings," he said dully, rolling his eyes for emphasis.

"Anything else?"

"Nope. You're dating a pretty boring guy, Elise."

Jasmine and Elise exchanged glances and then Elise said with exaggerated tact, "Don't you have some work to do somewhere?"

"I was just trying to help."

"Which I appreciate." Elise slid another catalog toward her as Chad disappeared around the corner of the nearest stack. "This is why I hate birthdays early in the dating process."

"Maybe you should just take him out," Jasmine said. "Dinner…drinks."

"I could buy him flowers."

"Get real," Chad called from the other side of the stacks.

Jasmine nodded in agreement. "No flowers."

"All right. Dinner."

TONY KNEW JASMINE HAD to be in the library somewhere, but he forced himself to focus on his reason for
being there. When Dorothy Murdock had called and
asked to meet with him on his day off, it had surprised
the hell out of him. He'd wondered for one wild moment
if she was going to warn him away from Jasmine.

He climbed the stone steps to the entrance, smiled a
little as he remembered borrowing the model-shipbuild-
ing book. Things hadn't gone so well with the ship, but
they'd become rather interesting with the person who'd
scanned the book for him.

Dorothy was waiting inside behind the big wooden
checkout desk, looking like a prim little bartender in her
white blouse with the bow at the neck.

"Good afternoon, Officer DeMonte," she said, stepping out to meet him. She gestured toward her office,
which was situated behind a frosted glass door with an
honest-to-goodness transom over the top. Tony surveyed the area as he walked. The library was a nice
place, with all the naturally finished woodwork and
overstuffed chairs for people to lounge in as they read.
No wonder Jasmine liked her job. It took place in a
good environment.

"Please have a seat." Dorothy waited until he was
situated in a dark oak chair that could have come
straight out of the principal's office he used to visit on
occasion, before she closed the door and then walked
to the center of the room, her movements deliberate, like
that of a litigator. "What do you know about the history
of this area?"

He felt his eyebrows go up. "Not a lot."

"Let me provide some background before I explain

why I called you." She stepped closer to her desk and picked up a book, which she handed to him. It was an old journal. Perplexed, he took it as she continued to speak. "Many of the houses in this neighborhood, like this library, were built at or close to the turn of the last century."

Tony nodded, carefully holding the old book, knowing this meeting was going somewhere, but not quite understanding how it tied into anything.

"The majority of the people who lived here during that time made their living in one of three ways—logging, mining or transporting goods to and from the seaports by way of the river." She looked at him sharply, as if attempting to discern his level of understanding.

Tony nodded. Good history lesson so far. Just as well he had nothing better to do on his day off. Jasmine was at work, and the lawn mowing was done.

Dorothy went to the window then and scanned the neighborhood. The library was situated on a small hill, allowing a view of the street and most of the houses to the south.

"Something is going on in the house across the street from the one on which you served the search warrant."

Tony instantly perked up as Dorothy continued musingly. "Are you familiar with Prohibition tunnels?"

"Prohibition tunnels?" Tony repeated, getting to his feet and joining her at the window, still holding the book.

"Yes. They were quite common for a time. The miners were adept at building them and the river provided a way to move large quantities of alcohol to and from the area. I gather that quite a few families helped make ends meet during hard times by brewing gin and such. A few got rich." She pointed to the old house across the street. "That house belonged to the Stewarts."

And now it belonged to Robert Davenport, as did the house they had raided the night Tony first met Jasmine.

"The same Stewarts the street is named after?" Tony rested a hand on the oak molding and leaned forward to get the full view from Dorothy's promontory.

"Yes. They were poor before Prohibition. He is said to have struck it rich with a mining claim that he subsequently sold, but upon reading some of the diaries and journals in our local history archives, I think the old coot was running gin and I think he had a tunnel. It's hinted at rather blatantly in the entries in that journal you are now holding." She smiled grimly. "My grandparents never liked the Stewarts."

"What's been happening, Dorothy?" Tony asked, cutting to the chase. He didn't have time to read an old journal and decipher blatant hints.

"I've been watching the neighborhood since the night we met in the alley."

Met in the alley. Interesting way of putting it.

"There haven't been a lot of comings and goings from the house you searched, as there had been before that incident, but three days ago, I witnessed an odd thing. I was here, drinking my morning coffee and watching the neighborhood as I was planning the day. I saw a man go into the Stewart house, but—" she raised her eyebrows in a significant expression "—he exited about fifteen minutes later from the side door of the house across the street, the one you searched that night."

Tony looked out the window again. She had an excellent view of the front of both the Stewart house and the alleged drug house.

"You can understand that, with all that shrubbery, he probably felt he was out of sight."

Unless he was being spied on by an old lady on the upper floor of a library. "He never exited the Stewart house?"

"No. It is possible he left another way and somehow entered the other house through a back door, but…why? When they are directly across the street from each other? Front door to front door makes much more sense."

Why, indeed?

And this would explain why the house had been so clean when he and Yates had searched it. The stuff could have been shuffled elsewhere—like the Stewart house— subterraneously. And tunnels were not that uncommon in Seattle and Portland. Why not here?

Tony gave the older woman an appraising look and then handed her the journal. "We'll see what we can find. Thank you. This…helps."

"I can't take all the credit. I wouldn't have thought of this had it not been for Andy. He's been researching the architectural history of the area and recently asked me about references that indicated which houses or neighborhoods might have had Prohibition tunnels. As soon as I saw that man coming out of the wrong house, I began to investigate."

Thank goodness for Andy the architectural history buff.

"I'll check into it." Or rather Yates would. Tony was an official short-timer now. One more week and then off to Seattle.

Tony arrived home feeling tired, but oddly satisfied.

He'd clued Yates in on Dorothy's theory. Yates latched on to the idea eagerly, making Tony believe that his friend had been an avid Hardy Boys reader.

But Dorothy might have something. It wasn't out of the realm of possibility. Now the big trick was to get enough information to convince a judge to sign another search warrant. Or perhaps one for both residences. But again that would be Yates's baby.

JASMINE WAS BEAUTIFUL in the morning. Tony propped himself up on his elbow and studied her as she slept, all too aware that soon he'd be waking up alone again. He wasn't going to dwell on it.

Jasmine's eyes opened then and she smiled sleepily. He caught her hand, which was already traveling south, and brought it up to kiss the tips of her fingers. "I've got to go to work."

She let out a groan. "Play hooky."

"Miss Responsibility wants me to lie about being sick?" And if they weren't shorthanded, he would have done so.

"Please?"

She pulled her hand free and trailed it down his abdomen, where she made a pretty convincing argument for staying. He needed most of his willpower not to yield. He rolled over on top of her, pinning her. He recognized challenge in her eyes and brought his forehead down to touch hers.

"I. Have. To. Go. To. Work," he said sternly.

"Who's stopping you?"

"Me. And you're not helping." She smiled with delight.

He kissed her deeply, and then, since he was rock hard and because it was the only way he'd eventually escape, he reached down to ease himself inside her. In Jasmine's house, you didn't leave until the landlady was satisfied.

She sighed. A sigh that made him glad to have given in. And then he proceeded to do what Jasmine had assured him he did better than anyone. From the way she responded, he was close to believing her. When he finally got out of bed, feeling better than he had in recent memory, he knew Jasmine was right. This was the proper way to start a day.

WITH LESS THAN A WEEK left at work, and therefore less than a week left at Jasmine's place, it was time for Tony to put his affairs in order, and that meant another trip to the garden store. By seemingly mutual agreement, he and Jasmine did not talk about the future—or the day when he'd be moving out.

And that was a good sign. They were both still playing by their original rules. They'd have their time together and then go their own ways. Because, as much as he cared for Jasmine—and he cared deeply—he didn't know a lot about having a long-term relationship—unlike his father, who'd been married to his present wife a couple of decades.

Permanence, suburbia, minivan. All foreign words, and he didn't have much confidence in his ability to learn the language, even if his finances and career were more suited to commitment.

THE GUY AT THE GARDEN shop loved Tony, since Tony bought big-ticket items—bushes and such—and he did it often.

"What do we need to replace today?" the man asked.

"Nothing."

The man's face fell.

"But I'd like to buy two lilacs, a pink rosebush and a whole bunch of daffodil bulbs." He was going to leave Jasmine with a lot of flowers in the spring and she'd told him that she loved daffodils. He was glad she liked a flower that was so easy to find and plant. And when they bloomed up in the spring, he hoped she remembered him fondly.

"Is that all?"

Tony started to nod and then stopped. The garden gnome in the corner looked very much as if he needed a home. Something else for Jasmine to remember him by—maybe something more apropos than flowers. "I'll take the gnome."

"Lester? You bet!"

TONY WAS DIGGING HOLES for the bushes when his phone rang. He didn't recognize the number, but he answered anyway.

"Are you living with my daughter?" Richard Storm asked as soon as he ascertained that he was indeed speaking to Tony DeMonte, the man he'd met at the awards reception.

"I'm renting the basement." And sleeping with her, but it wasn't officially living together, since they had separate closets and bathrooms and he was moving out in a matter of days.

There was a silence and then Tony heard the older man draw in a breath. "I was misinformed."

Gee. Wonder who did that?

"Jasmine's almost thirty," Tony felt compelled to point out.

"She's still my daughter."

"Yes."

"Do you have any children?"

"No."

"Then you wouldn't understand."

Tony had no comment.

"Why are you renting Jasmine's basement?"

"I lost my lease, and after the guy attacked Jasmine—"

"Attacked her!"

Hadn't she told him? Tony rubbed his hand over his face, tempted to end the call before he mucked things up any more than he had.

"I think he was just trying to get away."

There was another pause before Jasmine's father said, "Tell me the truth. Was she hurt?"

"Black eye. Bruised face."

Mr. Storm uttered an oath. "She told me a thief had been hiding in the garage and pushed her aside as he escaped."

"That's kind of true. He did that. He also landed on top of her and elbowed her in the eye. She probably wanted to keep from worrying you."

"And then *you* moved in."

"Yeah. I've been here ever since it happened."

"I guess I'm grateful to you."

"No problem," Tony said, thinking this was one of the weirder conversations he'd had in recent memory, although every conversation he had with Val came close to qualifying.

"And I apologize for being…stiff…at the reception. I didn't realize…please accept my apologies."

"Accepted," Tony said. *Stiff. Right.* More like… Tony squelched the thought. The guy was Jasmine's father.

"Thank you." A second later the line clicked dead, leaving Tony to hope that he hadn't made things worse between Jasmine and her old man.

"WHAT IS THAT?" Jasmine asked. She'd come into the backyard to find Tony on his knees, industriously planting bulbs and a hideous little garden gnome leering at her from between two bushes.

"You don't like it?"

"It's kind of…" The word *repulsive* died on her tongue. "Funky."

"Yeah." He nodded with satisfaction. "It is."

"What are you planting?"

"Daffodils," he said, unaware that he'd made her heart jump.

"And the bushes?"

"Two lilacs. An older house like this should have lilacs. I don't know why it doesn't." He returned to his digging.

"There's a rosebush, too."

"Yeah."

Jasmine returned to the house, glancing out the window at the man down on his hands and knees, the gnome grinning at her over his back.

How could you not love a man who had a thing for garden gnomes?

She couldn't, and she was going to demonstrate her gratitude for the ugly gnome in the way that Tony most appreciated.

TONY DROVE TO SEATTLE early the next morning, leaving before Jasmine went to the library. He had to talk to his superior about the assignment the powers-that-be had in mind for him. He just wished he felt more enthusiastic about a paying job. And that he hadn't found it so hard to drive away from the place he was starting to think of as home, even though he shouldn't be.

How had he allowed himself to slip so deeply into this imaginary life that bore no relations to his real life?

But how could he have predicted how difficult it would be to leave it, when he'd never experienced such a thing before?

About an hour before his meeting, he pulled into the parking lot of the condo he was in the process of buying for his mom.

"Hi," he said when Myra answered the door. Her eyes widened, and she pushed a hand through her short gray hair.

"Tony. Come on in." She stepped back to let him into the condo. "I didn't realize you were in town."

"I'm here to talk to Parker about the job."

"And…"

"We meet in an hour." Tony walked in, glanced around. Magazines and crossword puzzle books covered the two end tables and filled a basket next to a chair, but other than that the place was neat. Almost bare.

"Where's your furniture?"

"I sold the stuff I didn't need."

"Going to buy more?"

"I have enough for me." Two chairs, two stools at a breakfast bar, two end tables. Well, it did free up some space in the cramped room. He couldn't believe the amount he was paying per square foot for this place.

"You didn't sell the stuff because you needed money, did you?" he asked, watching her face as he spoke.

"Of course not. Hungry?"

Tony smiled. Funny question from someone who didn't cook.

"I have Oreos," she said.

"Then I'm hungry."

She disappeared into the kitchen and returned a few minutes later with the package of Oreos, a carton of milk and two plastic glasses.

"Cookies and milk," she said with satisfaction. "I quit drinking coffee, you know."

He hadn't.

"It aggravated my breast fibroids."

Tony managed to nod instead of choke. "Probably a good thing you quit, then."

"Yeah." She settled in the chair opposite his. "*You* aren't quitting, are you?"

Tony glanced up, perplexed for a moment before he picked up on her line of reasoning. "The department?"

"Yes. The department... You don't seem too enthused about going back."

He reviewed their last conversations and, yeah, he probably hadn't sounded that jazzed about hitting the streets again. And his mom was an expert at reading between the lines.

"I didn't quit until I reached mandatory," Myra added, grabbing another cookie. Fat lot of good it had done her. She was as broke now as she would have been had she quit earlier.

"I can't afford to quit."

"But you like law enforcement, right?"

"I did." He picked up one of her puzzle books, which was folded open. The puzzle was a four-star, almost completely done. His mother was good at puzzles. Unfortunately.

"Did?"

"Yeah." He looked up at her. "I did. Now I consider it…time well spent."

"Time well spent," Myra said flatly.

"I make a difference." His contribution may have been a drop in the bucket, but it was a drop that wouldn't have been there without him. "I gotta tell you, though. Toward the end of that last job, pressure started to wear on me. And after what happened with Gabe…sometimes I consider trying something else." He couldn't believe he was saying what he barely ever let himself think. To his mother, no less.

"What happened with Gabe wasn't your fault."

Not according to Val.

"And besides," his mother continued, "you don't know anything else. You're too old to change careers."

"Hey. As long I can swing the condo payments and a big bag of dog food—"granted, some months he found it tight to do, with his own rent added "—a job is a job."

"Not for me it wasn't." She bit into the Oreo.

"Yeah. I know." Her job was her life, whether she had a kid or not.

For a moment they stared at each other. She realized she wasn't a candidate for Mother of the Year, but she wasn't going to apologize for putting her job first. And Tony wasn't going to ask her to. He'd had a different kind of childhood. Not exactly normal or happy, but it had toughened him up. Got him ready for the streets.

Myra shook her head, her expression tight. She still held half the Oreo in her hand as she regarded her only off-spring—obviously wondering what was wrong with him.

Tony grabbed a couple of cookies—his lunch—then got to his feet. "Don't worry, Ma. I'll be gainfully employed and we'll get this condo paid off."

"I want you to like what you do." Correction. She wanted him to love police work the way she had.

Tony put a hand on his mother's shoulder and squeezed reassuringly, knowing these mother-son talks were as frustrating to her as they were to him. They were just too damn alike. Frightened by the same things—and in this case it was each other. But heaven help anyone who messed with mother or son.

An odd kind of love, but love it was.

"I should probably hit the road. I have to find a parking place and traffic is snarled up as usual."

"Will you be back?" Myra followed him to the door, and she looked as though she wanted him to come back—probably to reassure her that he was still a cop.

"I'll be trying to find a room to rent after the meeting."

Myra's eye narrowed. "Do you still own that night-mare of a dog?"

"Yep."

She hunched her shoulders. "Guess you aren't going to stay here."

"But maybe I'll try to come by more often."

Myra nodded solemnly. "You do that."

Tony waited until he was almost out the door before he said, "Love you, Ma."

Myra snorted, but Tony knew that was her way of saying *I love you, too.*

Time to meet with the boss, then find an apartment that would allow him to keep a nightmare dog.

CHAPTER THIRTEEN

THE MEETING WITH PARKER hummed along merrily and Tony felt pretty numb by the time he left the office, although he couldn't figure out why.

No. He did know why. It was because the meeting had driven home the fact that he was going back to work, thus putting an end to any ideas he had on the drive up to Seattle of taking a chance and asking Jasmine if she wanted to stay in contact and see what happened.

He could just hear the conversation now: *Hey, I'm broke and I hate the job I have to keep to buy the condo I can't live in, and oh, by the way, I'll be gone for six months. Did I mention that I think I love you?*

Yeah. He was a prize.

But this was how his life usually worked out—jamming him between the proverbial rock and hard place. With the condo and what was left of his credit rating hanging in the balance, he didn't have a lot of choice *but* to go back to work, and he wasn't going to embarrass himself by trying to elbow his way further into Jasmine's life. He'd just slip off into the night—the way a good narc should.

JASMINE HAD KNOWN THIS moment was coming—with the differences in their temperaments, their lifestyles, it was inevitable.

But that didn't make it any easier. Facing reality after she'd been having so much fun in fantasyland was hard.

But now that the moment was here, she was going to be matter-of-fact and logical. Her time with Tony had been spectacular, but she'd gone into the situation expecting it to be temporary. Could it be otherwise?

It's working pretty well now...

She kicked a pebble, shoved her hands deeper in her pockets as she and Tony walked through the park.

"So you're going to Spokane." She was amazed at how normal she sounded. As if his leaving didn't matter, when actually it was tearing her up inside.

"I don't have a lot of choice."

"You don't want a lot of choice." An observation, not a challenge. And although he was startled for a moment, he took it as such. They were being so civilized. Too civilized, considering the wild responses they were capable of evoking from each other in bed. Possibly because neither of them knew how to deal with the fact that the thing they had between them had become deeper than expected. Much deeper. To Jasmine, civility was the safest way *not* to deal with it just yet. She imagined that Tony was operating from the same motivation.

Tony stroked her hair and cupped the back of her neck. He needed to touch her and she needed to feel him, even if his touch was different, more impersonal.

"I have to work, Jasmine."

"The last I heard, people could have relationships and jobs."

Where had *that* come from? Her self-control was definitely crumbling.

"I would disappoint you eventually, you know. Right now…it's all new. And fun. But wait until I cancel plans over and over again because I have to work. Or I get beat up bad. Or some jerk shows up at the house looking for me because I arrested him."

"Yes. I'm too shallow and wimpy to deal with those types of issues." Why was she arguing with him?

Because she didn't want him to disappear from her life. Plain and simple.

"That isn't what I meant," he said calmly. He was obviously not going to be baited into anger. No doubt because of his years of experience controlling himself in dicey situations. "I've seen what happened with other cops I know. My mom and dad. Even Yates and Melanie have their issues."

What couple doesn't?

She swallowed the retort, gathering the remains of her self-control.

She had to take time to think before acting, but ultimately she wasn't about to let him just walk out of her life. Not without a fight anyway.

JASMINE WAS QUIET the day Tony packed his belongings into his car. He was leaving the bed behind and she'd agreed to keep Mutt until Tony found a place where he could keep him, so he didn't have all that much to stow. He'd slammed the trunk shut, then turned to find her leaning her shoulder against the gatepost, watching.

"It'll be different around here."

"Yeah. I imagine it'll be calmer."

"I'm not necessarily a big fan of calm anymore," she said.

"You were before I moved in."

"Yes. I guess I was. I didn't know what I was missing back then." She compressed her lips. "So this is it?"

There was a world of meaning in the words.

"This is it," he agreed.

She walked toward the car, Mutt dogging her steps, and stopped directly in front of him. When she looked up at him, he knew that the moment of truth had arrived—the one he'd hoped to avoid because he never ever wanted to hurt her.

"Do you think," she asked thoughtfully, "it's possible that we could make it, you and I?"

He looked into her beautiful eyes and said what was in his heart, because believing in a fantasy wouldn't help matters now.

"No," he said softly.

He could tell she didn't like that answer. Not one bit, but her voice only wavered slightly when she said, "Why not?"

"Because there's too much to change." And he had so little to work with. "I am not only flat broke, I'm in debt. All my savings went to bail my mom out of her bind. I have to keep this job because I'm not qualified to do anything else. If I take a job with another city— say, Mondell—I'm back to rookie pay. I live paycheck to paycheck as it is. Barely."

She nodded, her expression unreadable. "So it comes down to money."

Did it? No. It wasn't that simple, but he didn't know how to explain himself.

"I have my pride, Jasmine. I can't go into a relationship with nothing to offer. It would eat at me. And I don't want a job where I have to wear a paper hat. The job I do have is not one that's easy to share."

She bit the edge of her lip, glanced down at the ground. He hoped he hadn't seen the glint of tears.

"Jasmine, you thrive on organization. How organized would your life be with me around all the time?"

She didn't answer.

"Jas—"

When she looked up, her eyes were clear. No tears. Maybe this entire conversation had been based on a hypothetical question and he'd made a fool of himself.

"I think your reasoning is faulty."

His jaw dropped. "How so?"

"We could make it," she said stubbornly. "I think you're making excuses."

"And I think you're reading too much into the past few weeks."

Damn, that was an ugly thing to say, but from the suddenly frozen expression on her face, it had worked. "Jasmine, I—"

Don't fix it, he warned himself. He didn't have to.

"You've made your point," Jasmine said calmly. "I understand your position." She took a couple of steps backward. "Take care, Tony. I'll see you when you come back to get the dog."

And then she turned and walked to the house.

"YOU SHOULD HAVE been there! It was beautiful!"

Yates was so excited he was gesturing with his beer. It sloshed onto his pant leg, but he barely noticed. "I mean, you should have seen Davenport's face when we served the warrant on both places! He knew we knew, but you could see that he was still hoping that maybe we wouldn't find it."

Tony smiled and raised his glass in a salute before drinking. He'd thought that when Yates had asked him to meet at No Regrets after Yates's shift, it would be for a farewell beer. Turned out it was also for a congratulatory beer.

"How did you find the passage?" Tony asked, trying to focus on Yates's story instead of on Jasmine and what he'd just done.

Yates put his beer down with a thump and leaned across the table. His eyes were wide, and seemed to get wider as he continued the story. "I had a talk with that Andy kid at the library. You know, the one Dorothy said was the architect nut? He had some ideas on what to look for. There was this wire coming out of the wall next to the hot-water tank in the Stewart house and I swear, that door was twelve, maybe eighteen inches thick."

All of this, and Melanie was pregnant, too. Yates's life seemed to be falling into place just as Tony's was disintegrating more. But he'd never had any illusions of his life falling into place. He was a loner by both nature and circumstances. He had loved his time with Jasmine and, at the risk of sounding hokey, would cherish the memory. But all it would be was a memory. More for her sake than for his, whether she flipping believed him or not. Frankly, she was taking his departure well. Almost too well. Which told him that it was indeed for the best.

THE HOUSE FELT DIFFERENT without Tony, and Jasmine had to remind herself that she'd lived there quite happily for over a year before he'd moved in. There was no reason she couldn't continue to do that, except that she now knew what she was missing.

And she was missing it a lot.

She found Mutt's presence oddly comforting. She'd expected another round of digging as an expression of anxiety after Tony left, but it hadn't happened. Instead, the dog lay under the tree, chin on his paws, looking depressed. Jasmine knew the feeling.

She called Mutt in every night as Ghengis went out, and Jasmine paid him special attention when the cat wasn't around. Between the two animals, Jasmine was never alone—which was good, because she was darned tired of being alone.

She creased open her new planner. Only a week old and it did not yet have that old friend feeling, but she couldn't find her other one and was wondering if its disappearance was another incident she could file under "poltergeist."

She started a weekend to-do list, and on the top was "appliance store," where she would price new washers, since hers was finally about to give up the ghost. Both Dorothy and Andy had recommended the same store when she'd asked for advice, so that was the one she'd go to.

Below "appliance store" she wrote "garden store." She was going to buy Lester the garden gnome a friend. He needed someone to leer at besides her. And just because she was lonely, why should he be?

She flipped the book shut. She was without a doubt losing her mind.

Damn cop.

JASMINE'S PHONE RANG the next day just after she'd gotten home from work. She dropped her sweater on the chair and answered on the third ring. Her dad's number showed on the caller ID and she felt a surge of disappointment. Another award, maybe? Well, at least it gave them some contact. They'd exchanged a few terse e-mails since the night she'd spoken her mind, but this was the first call.

"Hello, Jasmine. I'm phoning to see how you're doing."

And…

It took her a moment to realize that was all.

"I, um, am doing fine. Why do you ask?"

"I thought you might be nervous living alone. Now that Tony has moved out."

"How do you know that Tony *has* moved out?" Or that he was living there in the first place.

"We talked. He didn't mention it?"

Jasmine's eyes grew round. Tony and her father had talked? "No. What did you talk about?"

"The man who was hiding in your garage, for the most part."

Jasmine waited a moment, then said, "That's all?"

"What else did you expect?" her father asked with the cool note he used when questioned.

"I'm not certain," Jasmine said wearily. "Like maybe you warned him off?"

"I didn't."

"Oh."

"I think…" Her father hesitated, which was very un-characteristic. "If I gave him a chance, I might like him."

Jasmine's jaw didn't drop. It plummeted. "But… he's not a college graduate and he doesn't know a bull from a bear."

"Neither do you and I like you." He cleared his throat. "I love you, actually," he added stiffly.

"I know that," Jasmine replied with equal huskiness. She searched for something to break the uncomfortable moment of silence that ensued. "I guess I was kind of hoping you'd warned him off. Then I'd have someone besides myself to blame for his leaving."

"There *is* something serious between you, then?"

"I thought you knew…" Sometimes her father made her tired. "Yes. I was hoping, anyway. But reality reared its ugly head and he's back working in Seattle and I'm here, pursuing my spinster lifestyle."

Her father made a noise that sounded amazingly like laughter.

"It's not funny," she grumbled.

"No. But…you remind me so much of your mother."

"I do?"

"I never let myself think about it before, but, yes, you do. She was prickly and guarded, but underneath, she was so warm and funny. It was just a matter of breaking through."

"I never knew she was like that. I only heard about what an amazing academic she was."

"Who would have told you, Jasmine?"

"You?"

"Yes. I should have. I—" His voice broke.

"Hey, Dad?" Jasmine said gently.

"Yes?"

"Instead of engaging in should-haves, why don't we engage in will-dos. You know, looking to the future instead of regretting the past?"

Jasmine unconsciously held her breath as she waited for her father's reply. "Yes. That's an excellent idea. Maybe in a few weeks I could manage a trip to Mondell that isn't connected with a business function."

"I'd like that." She plunged into the next question without allowing herself time to think. "Maybe you could tell me more about Mom. You and Mom were really different in temperament, then?"

"Quite."

"How did it work? No…would it have worked? Over the long term."

"No one can answer that."

"You never remarried."

"No," he said, obviously uncomfortable, and Jasmine realized that might be the answer to her question. "Now, if there's nothing else?"

"No. Nothing. Thanks for calling, Dad."

"Jasmine?"

"Yes?"

"I am here. If you need me."

"Thanks, Dad. I'll remember that."

Jasmine smiled philosophically as she put down the phone. She was finally figuring out how to connect with her distant father, it seemed.

At least that was something.

TONY TOOK ALMOST FIVE minutes to unpack his belongings in his new living space, a space that made Jasmine's basement appear palatial by contrast.

He felt right at home in the second-story studio apartment. And wished he didn't. He settled on the bed and reached into the box beside the rickety nightstand for the horticulture book he'd be returning to the library next trip to Mondell—he didn't want to mess with Dorothy—only, the book he pulled out of the box wasn't the library book. It was Jasmine's planner.

He weighed it in his hand for a moment before giving in to temptation and opening the cover.

Lists. Lots and lots of lists. Several on each day. Things to do. Things to buy. Things to achieve.

He smiled. That was Jasmine.

But as he continued to scan the pages, he began to notice something. The words were still neatly formed, the spacing perfect, but…the lists were shorter and there were fewer that involved everyday mundane activities and more that involved…well, dreams. Goals. And comments on small achievements. At the bottom of one list was the line item: *Forced to bowl. Must get revenge.*

Tony smiled again. She'd gotten it. He didn't even feel guilty as he turned the page. He found a grocery list there—but it was for lasagna. At the bottom of the list was a notation: *Research best noodles.*

The page for the day they'd first made love was…blank.

As was the next one.

His eyebrows rose. He'd upset her life enough to keep her from making her lists. Somehow he knew that was a good thing. There were a few notations over the past week—some of them numbered, but not nearly the precision battle plans she'd been making prior to his moving in.

Tony closed the planner slowly. Maybe it wasn't just

a matter of her completing him—maybe he completed her, and allowed her to let go of some of her control.

Maybe he was good for her in ways he hadn't even realized.

He flipped back to the Sean era, just to make sure. Lists. Straight, neat, each item either checkmarked off or rescheduled. Not one blank page.

Not even a recipe for lasagna.

IT WAS LATE WHEN he heard the light knock on his door. His cell phone rang almost simultaneously.

"It's me," Val said huskily. "Let me in."

"How'd you…" *Find me? More important, why'd you find me?*

As always, when Gabe was involved, he expected the worst. Wondered if he'd almost feel better once he'd heard the worst.

"I have my ways," Val said in answer to the unfinished question. The line went dead as Tony crossed the room to open the door. Val was leaning against the jamb on the other side, her phone still in her hand. She smiled, but it wasn't the hundred-watt smile she used to have. "Good to see you, Tony."

There was more than a little sarcasm in her greeting.

She remained strikingly attractive, with long red hair to the middle of her back, but some of the soft edges of her face had grown hard, and the black shirt she wore made her appear unnaturally pale. Life with her husband was taking its toll.

"How's Gabe?" Tony asked, stepping back to let her into the shabby room.

Val ignored the question as she casually walked

across the scarred linoleum to part the dingy window curtains. Outside was a wall three feet from the window.

"Nice view."

"You know I like the best."

"Since Gabe is in jail, he's not using so I guess he's okay," Val said in answer to his original question, turning then to lean on the sill, resting a hand on either side of her thighs. "And he won't be my responsibility for much longer." She glanced sideways, pressing her lips together, showing her profile.

"You're divorcing him?"

"I saw the lawyer today," she said with no sign of emotion.

Tony couldn't blame her for finally bailing. Gabe had twisted her life in knots. But he also didn't think it was a good time to be offering sympathy.

She looked back at him. "Maybe I should have stuck with you, Tony. You seem happy."

He laughed humorlessly. "You think I'm happy?" He'd like to *be* happy, but seemed incapable of allowing himself it. If he had, he would have figured out a way to stay with Jasmine.

"You're happier than me. Or Gabe." She moved off from the sill, sauntered toward him with a deliberate stride. "What do you say, Tony? Want to share a little of that happiness?"

Her expression was both detached and determined as she stopped in front of him and hooked her fingers possessively into the waistband of his pants.

Tony gently pulled her hands free. They were icy. She pulled them out of his grasp, let them drop to her sides.

"All right, you don't want me anymore. But…" She

tilted her chin up. "Do you ever miss me, Tony?" She spoke quietly. "Are you ever sorry I left you?"

"I was in the beginning," he said truthfully. "I was very sorry then."

"You were bitter then, too."

"Yes." No sense lying about it.

"Bitter enough to make certain that I was miserable, right?" There was a sudden bite to her voice.

He stiffened and moved back a step as he realized where she was heading.

"I did not encourage Gabe to apply to Narcotics in order to get back at you," he said, rubbing a hand over the side of his head.

"But you did encourage him."

Couldn't get around that. "I thought he'd be good at it." Tony had loved the job back then, and assumed his friend would love it, too. So when the opening had come up…

Val's expression was icy when she said, "You did more than that."

Tony's eyes flashed. "Shit, Val. What do you think I did?"

The coldness evaporated as she said, "You *knew* he had a problem and you encouraged him into a job that only made it worse. *And*—" her jaw tightened "—you had to know that would pretty much ruin *my* life, didn't you?"

"Val—"

"You two were always out carousing, but he ended up hooked and *you* didn't."

"You think that was part of my plan?" Tony asked incredulously. "Get real." He paced over to the door, which he now wished he'd never opened. "I tried to get him some help." As soon as he'd realized just how serious his partner's addiction was becoming. Gabe had not been cooperative.

"Oh, yeah. I *so* believe that." Val stood with her hands on her hips, chin jutting. "*You* made him what he is today, Tony, whether you planned it or not. You may as well have put that stuff up his nose *yourself*."

And that was the breaking point.

"I am *not* responsible for Gabe's decisions," Tony shouted, heedless of the fact that the older man in the apartment next door was probably trying to sleep. "You can say it all you want, but it isn't true."

And for the first time, the very first time, he found himself listening to the words: *He was not responsible.*

In hindsight, Gabe's heavy drinking obviously indicated a potential substance-abuse problem—and Tony had spent a lot of time beating himself over the head with that truth—but Tony'd had no way of knowing things would play out the way they did, when he'd encouraged his friend to apply for undercover work.

Gabe might have looked up to Tony, but that didn't make Tony responsible for Gabe.

He stepped forward to put his hands on Val's tense shoulders. "This isn't your fault. It isn't my fault."

She turned her head away. "I don't believe that."

"You should talk to someone, Val." And it clearly wasn't him.

"I'm not—"

"There are counseling resources I can hook you up with."

She sucked in a choking sob. "I don't need any damn counseling."

Tony begged to differ, but he'd fought enough with

Val to know it was useless to continue once she got like this. "Come on. I'll drive you home. Or better yet, to your sister's. Does Heather live at the same address?"

Val stubbornly clamped her lips together, but then, after taking another shaky breath, nodded. "I came here to hurt you tonight, Tony."

"Yeah," he said as he put an arm around her and led her to the door, "I kinda figured that out."

She leaned into him. "I want to be happy."

"So do I, Val."

The big question was—did he have any idea how to let himself do that without messing up someone else's life?

CHAPTER FOURTEEN

"SO ARE YOU GOING to Spokane or Mondell?" Myra asked.

Tony pulled his mother's car into the carport at the back of the condo building.

"Don't know." He'd called her to pick him up after dropping Val off at her sister's house, and by using some mother radar he hadn't even known she possessed, she had deduced that her son was troubled and it was because of more than Val.

And so he'd talked. A little. Told her walking away from Jasmine had been hard, even if it had been the sanest thing to do. But he hadn't mentioned thinking he might be in love with Jasmine. He'd let his mom figure some things out on her own.

"You don't know where you're going?"

"Nope." But he had a good idea. If he quit, it had to be soon, like yesterday, so they could get another guy on the task force. He knew he wouldn't do that. It was irresponsible. He might be a reprobate, but he was a responsible one.

"You remind me of your father."

"I'll get a haircut," he said automatically, removing the keys from the ignition, but making no move to get out of the car.

"No. Not the fact that you are his clone. The fact that you let a woman tie you in knots."

Tony stopped fiddling with the keys and cast a curious look her way.

"Who tied my father in knots?" He half expected her to open the car door and get out, since she wasn't one for discussing his father at length. But she stayed put.

"I did," his mother said in a quiet voice. "I tied him in knots and I didn't have to." And then she turned her head to stare out the passenger-side window. Tony was almost afraid to ask another question, afraid she'd clam up when he suddenly felt for the first time in his life that he needed some answers.

"I pretty much forced him to leave, you know."

"You kicked him out?"

"I made him miserable." She folded her hands in her lap, let out a breathy sigh. "I couldn't believe he was going to stay. So I tested him over and over again." She was quiet again before she added, "A guy can take only so much, you know, before he leaves."

He'd already been aware that the relationship had failed because of his mother, but he had assumed her devotion to her job had done it. Which was the impression she had worked to give him, but when he met her eyes, she was shaking her head.

"It wasn't the job. That came later. When I found that I'd tossed out the one man who was worth a…" She didn't finish with the colorful word Tony expected. She shrugged philosophically. "What can I say? I screwed up. He was a good man. But better off without me."

"How were you without him?" Tony had a hard time believing he was having this conversation, much less in a small Toyota with rapidly fogging windows. His taciturn mother was actually cutting loose with some information about stuff she *never* talked about.

"Lonely." She smiled ironically. "Surely you've figured out by now that I'm my own worst enemy. If it's something good or that will make me happy, I flush it down the dumper."

Tony turned the keys over in his hands. Over and over again. "If my dad was such a good man, then why didn't he want anything to do with me?"

"Did it ever occur to you that his wife might have had something to do with that? I mean, there you were, a clone of him, which his other boys were not, and a constant reminder of, well, me?"

Tony shook his head, uncertain whether his mother was being egotistical, or in possession of information he was not.

"And maybe you weren't the easiest kid to get along with, and headed to trouble to boot?"

"So what are you saying here, Ma?"

Her eyebrows came together in a way that suggested she might be about to slap some sense into him. He was right. "I'm *saying,* don't be stupid."

"Too late."

"Stop letting her tie you in knots. Find something worthwhile to focus on."

"Like a job?" Tony asked with an edge of irony.

"It worked for me," his mom said emphatically.

But it wouldn't for him. He knew that as clearly as he knew that his mother was incapable of sustaining a permanent relationship. The job was her relationship. The job was now a paycheck to him.

"Or I could go back to her. See if we could work something out." He voiced the idea, just to hear his mother's reaction.

"Think she'll have you?" his mother asked with a smirk.

Tony shook his head before glancing sideways. "You need to quit building up my confidence, you know?"

"Maybe I'm trying to piss you off so you'll do the right thing."

"What is that, Ma?"

"That's what I want you to tell me." She was tenser than he'd seen her in a long time. "Tony, there's one thing you need to know…"

"What's that?"

"After it was over, once and for all…well, that's the first time I felt like I was at peace. I didn't have to worry about losing him."

For a moment he just stared at her, and then a wave of sadness hit him. She was happy that the bad thing had happened because at last she could just deal with it.

And he hadn't been behaving a whole lot differently.

He paused with his hand on the door handle, then reversed course. He leaned over to kiss his mom's cheek, knowing he'd done the best she could—with him. With life.

And she was right. He was like his dad.

IT WAS ONE LONG NIGHT, and he spent it on his mother's floor with a blanket and pillow because he hadn't wanted to head back to the hellhole he was calling home.

He'd had myriad opportunities for deep reflection over the years—stakeouts, patrols, waiting for his turn at the

Department of Motor Vehicles—but he'd never actually analyzed his life as he did that night lying on the hard floor, listening to the squeaking footsteps of the insomniac pacing the floor of the condo directly above him.

Up until that point, he'd largely endured the parts of his life he didn't like, never realizing how those parts had multiplied or how hard they made it to share his life with someone else, with the exception of a big dog.

He could see that he'd been using those parts as a shield, because they gave him an excuse to walk away. *My life is a mess. Stand back. Avoid entry.*

Pride had gotten in the way, too, just as he had confessed to Jasmine. Even when he was willing to open his heart, risk his emotions, he was too embarrassed to offer his life the way it was. Too much sacrifice required, and he couldn't do that to someone he loved.

And he'd been absolutely convinced that he couldn't change. That he was destined to live the life he had, maybe because that was what he'd watched his mother do. No telling.

I want to be happy.

Val's statement kept popping into his mind, along with his mental echo that he wanted to be happy, too. Why *shouldn't* he be happy? It was his life, after all. His only one.

So was it possible to change things at this late date?

He could try. If he didn't make a move now, then he'd end up like his mom, doing crossword puzzles and taking a weekly bus down to the shooting range. Only, he wouldn't like it the way she did.

And he was not going to make the other mistake his mother had made. If he and Jasmine tried to have a relationship and then Jasmine decided she wanted to leave, she could, but he was not going to drive her away because he assumed her leaving was inevitable.

TONY KNEW HE NEEDED some kind of a plan. He couldn't approach a compulsive list maker without a list of his own. His initial attempt was a bit sketchy—definitely not up to Jasmine standards. It was, however, the best he could come up with on short notice.

He worked on refining it on the drive down to Mondell, where he planned to pick up his dog, drop off Jasmine's planner and find the library book, but he had a feeling he'd actually have to put his idea on paper before he felt comfortable with it.

He was becoming Jasmine.

The big question was—how would Jasmine take this visit? He'd hurt her when he'd told her things couldn't work between them, but at the time, he'd spoken the truth. Now he had to make her believe a new truth.

Her cell phone was off, as per library regulations, so he left a message on her answering machine at home, hoping she'd check it and know that he was coming. If not, he'd stop by the library, test the waters…see if he had to commit the plan to paper.

He'd just prefer not to do it in front of Dorothy.

SO TONY WAS ON his way to Mondell to pick up the dog and drop off her missing planner.

Jasmine turned off her cell phone and pushed it down into her purse after checking messages at home. She did not have a doubt that he'd be gone long before she got home from work *and* that he'd read her planner.

She slung her purse over her shoulder and did the unthinkable—asked Dorothy for the rest of the day off, promising to work weekends until the end of the year to make up for it. She drove home, her heart beating faster, a dozen or more scenarios playing in her head. She wished she had a vague idea of what she wanted to say, but figured she'd know once she saw him.

The gate was slightly ajar when she arrived, and her heart sank. He'd already been there. She'd been tricky, but he'd been trickier. He must have driven hell-bent on election to have made it down from Seattle in that amount of time.

She let herself into the house and went straight to the basement, needing to see the empty room before she believed he was gone once and for all.

She rounded the corner at the bottom of the stairs and then stopped, stupefied. Her clothes dryer was moved out from the wall and the exhaust hose was disconnected.

A strange chill went through her as she began to realize just how wrong this was. Tony wouldn't have done this…and then she raised her eyes to find Andy standing in the shadows near the hot-water tank.

Their gazes connected, and for one frozen moment they stared at each other.

"This isn't what you think," Andy said.

"Oh?" Jasmine cut a quick glance toward the door, judging distance.

"No. I just need time. A little time. That's all."

"How much?" Jasmine asked, instinctively trying to keep him talking, even if it was crazy.

He did not reply. "I won't hurt you," he said, "but I have to make sure that you stay here. Until I'm gone."

Jasmine's breath was becoming shallow and uneven as panic rose. She swallowed hard, trying to keep her head, trying not to hyperventilate.

"I'll stay here," she said, wondering if he was insane or homicidal or what.

"I have to make sure of that." He pulled a knife out of his pocket, fixed his gaze on the clothesline.

Oh, dear heavens. Jasmine slowly took a step backward and his eyes jerked back to her.

"No. I won't hurt you. I promise."

Then why was he in her basement? Jasmine made a dash for the door, grabbed the handle and yanked, groaning in frustration as she realized it was dead bolted.

She fumbled with the bolt, managed to slide it open, just as Andy grabbed her hard, yanked her backward.

She jammed her elbow into his chest and twisted, losing her balance and stumbling sideways onto the stairs. Andy kept hold of her shirt and they both went down on the bottom step. The knife clattered to the floor.

"Stop it, bitch." Andy took a swing at her with his free hand just as a deep roar came from the backyard and Muttzilla hit the door, popping the flimsy latch. Andy's head swiveled around and his mouth gaped as the door banged open and the huge dog skidded to a stop, looking for his quarry.

Jasmine broke free as Andy instinctively loosened his grip, and then, since he was standing between her and the open door, she scrambled up the stairs, praying that the dog would eat the kid alive.

She was almost to the top, when she was brutally pushed forward and sent sprawling across the kitchen linoleum. Andy kicked at the dog, catching him in the chest and knocking the animal far enough down the stairs to allow him to close the door.

Jasmine scrambled on her hands and knees, trying to get to her feet on the slick floor, when Andy dove at her, grabbing her ankle, bringing her down. A lint-covered black bag slid past her on the waxed hardwood floor as she kicked backward, catching him in the chin and hearing a satisfying grunt of pain.

Seeking a weapon, any weapon, Jasmine grabbed for the remarkably heavy bag, and then regained her feet, crouching in a defensive position as she faced Andy.

Andy's eyes were on the bag in her hand. He wet his lips.

"Give it," he said in a low voice. His eyes were now cold, oddly empty. "Give it to me or I *will* hurt you."

And so Jasmine gave it to him. She wound up and pitched the bag straight at him, hitting him square between the eyes.

Jasmine was out of the house before he hit the ground.

She raced blindly down the walk to the gate, running smack into a solid wall of man and letting out a small scream as his hands closed over her shoulders.

MUTT CAME RIPPING around the house just as Jasmine barreled into Tony, nearly knocking him over. Only, the dog ignored his faithful owner, and instead bounded up the porch steps and charged in through the open front door. Tony took Jasmine by the arm and hauled her to his car, where he opened the center console to retrieve his weapon.

"Get in and lock the doors. Who's in the house?"

"Andy."

"Alone?"

"Yes."

"Armed?"

"He had a knife." Tony grabbed for his phone from the dashboard.

"Number two, speed dial," Jasmine said, taking the phone from him. Her fingers were ice-cold.

"Lock the doors. Drive away if you have to."

As Tony cautiously approached the house, the only sounds he could hear were the dog's nails on the hardwood floor and intermittent moaning. He pushed shrubbery aside to take a quick look through the living-room window before entering the house, his weapon ready.

He didn't need it. Andy was just struggling to a sitting position, groaning as he held his head. Muttzilla was facing him, the ridge on his back up, his teeth bared, just daring Andy to try something.

Andy must have reminded Mutt of his former owner.

WHEN BACKUP ARRIVED, Tony went out to Jasmine, and held her against him as they sat side by side on the step. Neither of them spoke. After they had transported Andy, Tony accompanied Jasmine to give her statement, and then they hung around while the investigating officer questioned Andy.

It took the officer almost an hour to get the story. Andy didn't want a lawyer, but he didn't want to provide many details, either.

Possibly because Andy was not Andy—or not the Andy he'd pretended to be. And his father was not a teacher. His father was in prison and his grandmother had once owned Jasmine's house.

That was where the story took a sharp turn into the realm of the unusual.

The velvet bag did not hold drugs but instead contained the biggest chunk of gold any of them had ever seen. And no one—not even Andy—had a clue where the gold had come from. Andy's father had quite possibly stolen it prior to his arrest on an unrelated charge. What *was* clear was that he'd given it to his mother for safe-keeping, directing her to hide it in the house and not to tell a soul the nugget existed, especially the family; he didn't trust them not to rat him out and steal his nugget.

Andy's grandmother had followed instructions and then unexpectedly passed away several months later. The surviving family members sold the house, having no idea that a fortune resided in the walls. They'd made a nice profit on the sale, and as far as they knew, all was well—except that Andy's father was in prison and his nugget was now hidden in someone else's house. He'd had no choice but to contact Andy and tell him the story before Jasmine stumbled across the nugget in the midst of a renovation or found it due to dumb luck.

So Andy had simply become the library volunteer. He had access to Jasmine's keys, which she kept in her purse in the staff room, and knew her schedule. When she'd changed locks, he'd had a copy of her new key made during his lunch break.

The only problem was that he'd had a hell of a time figuring out where an old woman would hide a fist-size gold nugget—until Jasmine had told him a few days ago that the appliances were hand-me-downs.

"I'M SO DAMN SORRY I didn't believe you." Tony poured Jasmine a cup of water from the cooler at the back of the squad room and then handed it to her along with the aspirin she'd requested.

Her hands shook slightly as she raised the cup to her lips, but her voice was steady when she said, "It's fine. There was no reason you should have. I mean, the guy was careful and the whole thing is kind of crazy." She quirked a corner of her mouth thoughtfully. "Totally crazy."

She looked at him as if she could apply that description to other things she'd recently done—like sleeping with him. Jasmine was coming to her senses and he felt a stab of desperation.

He no longer wanted to be selfless here. He wanted to hold her close, make up for leaving when she'd needed him.

"Hey." Yates strolled in, practicing perfect timing. "You doing all right?" he said, with a hand on the back of Jasmine's chair, and open concern on his face. Tony understood, but he also wanted to be alone with her.

"Better," Jasmine said with an attempt at a smile. She tilted the glass, finished the water. Yates reached for the cup and she handed it to him.

"Your ride is here, so any time you're ready…"

"Great." Jasmine rose to her feet. "Thanks. You've been great."

She spoke quietly, and did not seem to be including Tony in her gratitude.

Tony walked with her to the glass exterior doors. Her hand was on the release bar when he said, "Can I stay with you tonight?" He'd been hoping for an invitation, but it obviously wouldn't be extended.

Her eyes jerked up to his. "I can take care of myself."

"I'm not staying with you to keep you safe."

"Or out of guilt because you didn't believe me and weren't there to protect me?" she asked coolly.

"Jasmine—"

"I don't want to talk right now, Tony. Dorothy's waiting for me. I have to go." She pushed the door open and walked outside to where Dorothy's car was waiting in the lot, leaving Tony alone.

"She's in shock," Yates commented when Tony came back into the room, feeling like kicking a garbage can or something.

"She's pissed."

"That, too." And then Yates put his head down and started typing.

"I WAS DATING A PSYCHO," Elise said for the ninth or tenth time.

"More of a calculating and desperate person who was trying to find a fortune," Dorothy said soothingly, handing Elise a mug of ginger tea.

Jasmine sat in an overstuffed chair, her feet curled up under her. *If he'd indicated that he wanted to try to make something with her before he left, it would be different.* But he'd flat out told her things would never work between them only a matter of days ago, and as much as she'd love to spend the night with him, she wasn't going to out of a sense of duty or fair play. Or to make him feel better for a while because he *hadn't believed her.* The only thing that had changed was the fact that Andy had attacked her.

Tony's rationale for leaving still existed, and until it didn't, she'd do fine on her own, thank you very much.

"So he volunteered just because you worked at the library?" Elise said, referring to Andy and still dazed.

"He had to get my keys and he had to know where I was and when, because searching could require some time."

"And he was the reason that Ghengis was out."

"It's hard to keep Ghengis in unless you know the proper foot block." And she was pretty certain that Andy had been the one who'd caused Ghengis's injuries when the cat had been so stiff and sore. He'd probably kicked the cat to prevent him from escaping again.

"How's Tony taking all this?"

"I don't have the foggiest."

Elise frowned in disbelief.

"No, really," Jasmine said, "and I think it's best that we go our own ways now. He can do his renegade cop thing and I can stay here and do my thing." *I'll get over him.* And if she spent more time with him, she'd just hurt more when he left again.

Dorothy settled on the sofa and picked up her cup.

"That sounds lovely," she said. "And maybe while you're at it…" Jasmine looked up expectantly as Dorothy's voice trailed. "You could cut off your nose to spite your face."

The older woman smiled sweetly and took a long sip of tea.

THE LIGHTS WERE ON in her house. Jasmine had cajoled Dorothy into driving her home so that she could get Ghengis before spending the night in Dorothy's guest room.

The two women exchanged glances.

"I'll call the police." Dorothy reached for her phone, but Jasmine stopped her with a movement of her hand.

"I'm pretty sure that *is* the police," Jasmine said as she recognized the car at the curb.

"You mean…?"

"He probably doesn't want me to be alone."

"He's probably right," Dorothy said.

Jasmine inhaled deeply as she took hold of the door handle.

Dorothy put her hand on Jasmine's arm. "You're sure it's him?"

"Oh, yes," Jasmine said. "I'm sure."

Her heart was beating fast as she walked toward the house, mounted the steps to the porch. She paused with her hand on the door and then opened it. The heavenly smell of lasagna hit her nostrils. She followed it into the kitchen where Tony was standing at the sink, his hands deep in dishwater. She didn't want to think about how right he looked there, in her kitchen, because ultimately he wouldn't let himself stay.

He knew she was there, but he did not turn around.

"What are you doing here?"

"I have two more days of rent."

"I believe you were renting the basement," she said.

"Yes." He pulled his hands out of the water and dried them. When he faced her, he was more serious than she'd ever seen. "I never told you that I was in love with you, did I?"

Jasmine's heart skipped at his matter-of-fact declaration, but she ignored the reaction. "You said you cared." *And that you were sorry you didn't believe me.*

"That's not the same as saying you love someone." The expression in his dark eyes was intense, but Jasmine saw something else there. Uncertainty. Maybe even vulnerability.

"Then, no. You didn't tell me that." She couldn't believe how cold she sounded, but she wasn't ready to show her own vulnerabilities. "You *did* say we couldn't make it together."

"That's because I guess I'm of the old school. You know, the one where if you want to go into a relationship, you have to have something to offer—other than yourself. I don't. All I have is a shell of a life."

Jasmine opened her mouth, but he raised a hand, so she closed it and let him continue.

"But I will have something to offer eventually…which is what I came down here to tell you. I wanted you to know that. Just so…you could know," he finished lamely.

"I see." Jasmine felt herself starting to thaw, the first deadly step toward no going back.

He cleared his throat. "It's going to take time. Probably a couple of years. And then I'll be forty-four. And you'll probably have found someone else, and… well, I just can't let you do that without at least letting you know that I'll be working on a future, and it'll be in something where a woman wouldn't have to worry about me coming home at night and…" He gestured in frustration instead of finishing the sentence, and Jasmine realized she was doing more than thawing. She was melting.

Tony, who'd been so convinced that he was locked into his current life and incapable of change, was

making plans to change—plans that included her, if she
would have him.

"I can live with it," Jasmine blurted. "Your job, I
mean. The one you have now. I can live with it."

Tony's mouth flattened. "You shouldn't *have* to live
with it."

"But I *will*," she said quietly. "I don't want to have
to wait two years for you to make things perfect."

"Maybe I need to—"

"I hope not," Jasmine interrupted, and then, for one
long, tense moment, they studied each other from their
respective sides of the kitchen.

Her cocky cop was not looking at all cocky right
now—in fact, he hadn't looked cocky the past several
times she'd seen him.

"So…" he finally asked cautiously, gripping the
edge of the counter on either side of him, "are you
saying that maybe we should keep in contact while I
work on things?"

She crossed the kitchen, her steps deliberate, her
gaze fixed on his face, and watched his expression shift
from uncertain to…more uncertain. "Yes. We should
stay in contact. Close, close contact."

"Close contact, you say?" The smile she loved was
edging back onto the mouth she loved, and Jasmine felt
her insides turn to liquid.

She wound her arms around his neck then, needing
to touch him and feeling both amazed and grateful that
things were…somehow…working out. His hands hov-
ered for a moment before they settled at her waist.

"I think we should map out this plan of yours
together," she said. "Because I am very good at planning

and mapping, and, surprisingly, having you around only seems to increase the ordered feeling in my life, because having you here is right. And if you want your two years, you can have your two years."

His grip tightened on her waist, and for a long moment they stood holding each other, touching, being, until the timer went off for the lasagna.

"I still have to make a salad," he said.

"Why don't you put the lasagna in the warming oven, and we'll make a salad later." She touched her finger lightly to his bottom lip, her expression quite serious. "Much…much…later."

"Maybe," he said as he folded her against him, "we could even do without."

"I'm in agreement." She nuzzled the underside of his jaw. "As long as you're talking salad."

"I never was a big fan of lettuce—just ask Yates."

EPILOGUE

"NO," TONY SAID, rubbing a hand over his face. "You can't use that diameter tubing on the drip system. Go with one-fourth... Yes, I'm sure... Right... Call if you have more questions."

He hung up the phone and shook his head. "I'm never going to get him trained."

"But he likes working for you better than for the library."

"Lucky me." But he was smiling, and Jasmine went to perch on the edge of his chair. He wrapped an arm around her waist. "You want to do the monthly report?"

"Nope. I'm going to work, which is so much quieter without Chad."

"Come on...you miss him."

"A little." She smiled as she wrapped one of his curls around her finger. "He did bring us together." And she did hope her baby had his father's hair. In about seven months they'd find out.

"Yeah." Tony leaned back in his chair, pulling her with him. "And he likes to point that out when he wants an afternoon off."

"Which you, of course, give him."

"Of course. That was the first thing your father told

me when I received that impromptu business lesson—let the employees do whatever they want, when they want."

Jasmine nodded. "That sounds like Dad."

She was hearing from him a little more often now that a grandchild was in the offing. And he had helped them out by financing the garden store purchase and helping refinance the condo. Jasmine was developing a whole new appreciation for the business world as she became more deeply involved with it, though it wasn't as satisfying as the library.

Tony still met with Yates regularly, but he didn't seem to miss law enforcement. He'd put in his time, he told her late one night while they were lying in bed, watching Ghengis prowling the fence railing outside their window, looking for the perfect place to ambush the dog. And he'd done some good. But he wanted different things in life—he wanted some of the things he hadn't gotten much of as a kid. Like a family life. One that didn't consist solely of a big cat and a bigger dog.

The biggest surprise since they'd been together had come when Myra had gotten a roommate—another ex-policewoman—and the two of them had taken over the now-smaller condo payment. Tony still sent a check once a month to help tide Myra over, but it wasn't as huge as before, and this roommate didn't appear to have any pie-in-the-sky investment ideas. Jasmine suspected that Myra hadn't exactly wanted a roommate, but had taken one as a gift to her son—to help free him up so that he could pursue the next phase of his life.

And Jasmine appreciated that. Deeply. She snuggled closer.

"I thought you had to go to work," he pointed out, but his arms tightened.

The phone rang just then and Jasmine handed it to him.

"She wants what?... Yeah. We can do that. I'll do up a rough estimate and call you back in a few minutes... What?... I know what happened last time... Yes, I really mean a few minutes."

Jasmine pushed herself up off his lap. She, too, remembered what had happened last time, and knew that it had largely been her fault.

"I have to go," she said. But she was unable to make herself sound like she meant it.

He looked up, and she could hear Chad on the other end of the line, calling in a faint voice, "Please go..."

She smiled, then took the receiver out of her husband's hand and put it back in the cradle.

"You used to be so responsible," Tony said, as he once again pulled her down into his lap.

"Yes, I know. And I'll be responsible again—in about twenty minutes."

* * * * *

Here's a sneak peek at
THE CEO'S CHRISTMAS PROPOSITION,
the first in USA TODAY *bestselling author*
Merline Lovelace's HOLIDAYS ABROAD *trilogy*
coming in November 2008.

American Devon McShay is about to get the Christmas surprise of a lifetime when she meets her new client, sexy billionaire Caleb Logan, for the very first time.

Silhouette
Desire

Available November 2008

Her breath whistled out in a sigh of relief when he exited Customs. Devon recognized him right away from the newspaper and magazine articles her friend and partner Sabrina had looked up during her frantic prep work.

Caleb John Logan, Jr. Thirty-one. Six-two. With jet-black hair, laser-blue eyes and a linebacker's shoulders under his charcoal-gray cashmere overcoat. His jaw-dropping good looks didn't score him any points with Devon. She'd learned the hard way not to trust handsome heartbreakers like Cal Logan.

But he was a client. An important one. And she was willing to give someone who'd served a hitch in the marines before earning a B.S. from the University of Oregon, an MBA from Stanford and his first million at the ripe old age of twenty-six the benefit of the doubt.

Right up until he spotted the hot-pink pashmina, that is.

Devon knew the flash of color was more visible than the sign she held up with his name on it. So she wasn't surprised when Logan picked her out of the crowd and cut in her direction. She'd just plastered on her best businesswoman smile when he whipped an arm around her waist. The next moment she was sprawled against his cashmere-covered chest.

"Hello, brown eyes."

Swooping down, he covered her mouth with his.

Sheer astonishment kept Devon rooted to the spot for a few seconds while her mind whirled chaotically. Her first thought was that her client had downed a few too many drinks during the long flight. Her second, that he'd mistaken the kind of escort and consulting services her company provided. Her third shoved everything else out of her head.

The man could kiss!

His mouth moved over hers with a skill that ignited sparks at a half dozen flash points throughout her body. Devon hadn't experienced that kind of spontaneous combustion in a while. A *long* while.

The sparks were still popping when she pushed off his chest, only now they fueled a flush of anger.

"Do you always greet women you don't know with a lip-lock, Mr. Logan?"

A smile crinkled the skin at the corners of his eyes. "As a matter of fact, I don't. That was from Don."

"Huh?"

"He said he owed you one from New Year's Eve two years ago and made me promise to deliver it."

She stared up at him in total incomprehension. Logan hooked a brow and attempted to prompt a non-existent memory.

"He abandoned you at the Waldorf. Five minutes before midnight. To deliver twins."

"I don't have a clue who or what you're…"

Understanding burst like a water balloon.

"Wait a sec. Are you talking about Sabrina's old boyfriend? Your buddy, who's now an ob-gyn doc?"

It was Logan's turn to look startled. He recovered faster than Devon had, though. His smile widened into a rueful grin.

"I take it you're not Sabrina Russo."

"No, Mr. Logan, I am *not*."

* * * * *

Be sure to look for
THE CEO'S CHRISTMAS PROPOSITION
by Merline Lovelace.
Available in November 2008 wherever books are sold, including most bookstores, supermarkets, drugstores and discount stores.

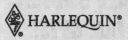

® HARLEQUIN®

American ★ Romance®

LAURA MARIE ALTOM
A Daddy for Christmas
THE STATE OF PARENTHOOD

Single mom Jesse Cummings is struggling
to run her Oklahoma ranch and raise her
two little girls after the death of her husband.
Then on Christmas Eve, a miracle strolls onto
her land in the form of tall, handsome bull
rider Gage Moore. He doesn't plan on staying,
but in the season of miracles, anything
can happen....

Available November
wherever books are sold.

LOVE, HOME & HAPPINESS

HAR75237

Silhouette®

Romantic
SUSPENSE

**Sparked by Danger,
Fueled by Passion.**

Lindsay McKenna
Susan Grant

Mission: Christmas

Celebrate the holidays with a pair
of military heroines and their daring men
in two romantic, adventurous stories
from these bestselling authors.

Featuring:

"The Christmas Wild Bunch"
by *USA TODAY* bestselling author
Lindsay McKenna

and

"Snowbound with a Prince"
by *New York Times* bestselling author
Susan Grant

Available November wherever books are sold.

COMING NEXT MONTH

#1524 SECOND-CHANCE FAMILY • Karina Bliss
Suddenly a Parent
The last thing Jack Galloway wants is to raise a family. But now he's guardian
of his late brother's three kids. What does a workaholic businessman know about
being a parent? Jack's about to find out when he discovers who his co-guardian is:
his ex-wife, Roz!

#1525 CHRISTMAS WITH DADDY • C.J. Carmichael
Three Good Men
Detective Nick Gray has made a career out of playing the field. But unexpected
fatherhood has put him to the ultimate test—and he needs help! Lucky for him,
Bridget Humphrey steps in as temporary nanny. Can this fun-loving bachelor
become a devoted family man? In the season of miracles, anything can happen!

#1526 COWBOY FOR KEEPS • Brenda Mott
Home on the Ranch
Cade misses how Reno used to look up to him, almost like a big brother. But
that was when he'd been a deputy sheriff—before he was forced to shoot her
stepfather…before he left town, abandoning Reno when she needed a big brother
most. Well, now he's back. And Reno needs his help, even if she's too proud to
admit it.

#1527 THE HOLIDAY VISITOR • Tara Taylor Quinn
Each Christmas, Craig McKellips stays at Marybeth Lawson's B and B. For those
intense days, their relationship grows. But it's jeopardized when he reveals his
identity...and his link to her past. Can she forgive the man who could be the love
of her life?

#1528 CHRISTMAS IN KEY WEST • Cynthia Thomason
A Little Secret
Abby Vernay's coming home for Christmas—to her eccentric family in Key West.
And to the man she's been avoiding for thirteen years. Now chief of police,
Reese Burkett is as irresistible as ever. But if they're going to have a future
together, she has to come clean about the past. And the secret she's been
keeping all this time.…

#1529 A CHRISTMAS WEDDING • Tracy Wolff
Everlasting Love
Their daughter's wedding should be among the happiest of days. Instead, Desiree
and Jesse Rainwater are barely holding their marriage together. She knows their
love is still strong and will do whatever it takes to prove to him they share too
much to walk away.

HSRCNMBPA1008